Exposed

Slocum spun, cocked his six-shooter, and froze. His finger had started back on the trigger when he saw a ghostly white figure coming toward him.

"What's going on, John?" Spring called. She hadn't bothered to put on any clothes other than her shoes. As fetching as it was seeing such a naked vision of beauty, Slocum snapped at her.

"Get down. Somebody's killed Jerome."

"Oh, really. That's ridiculous. Who'd—Oh my god, no!" She let out a shriek that could have been heard all the way back in Tombstone.

Slocum went to her and clamped his hand over her mouth.

"The killer's still out there." He tightened his grip on her as she began struggling. He had no other choice but to keep her quiet or she was going to put them both in jeopardy.

Jerome had fought, and it hadn't done him any good. Slocum wasn't going to die as easily—and he wasn't about to let the naked Spring Atkins die that way, either.

JAKE LOGAN

SLOCUM
AND THE
FOUR SEASONS

J
JOVE BOOKS, NEW YORK

THE BERKLEY PUBLISHING GROUP
Published by the Penguin Group
Penguin Group (USA) Inc.
375 Hudson Street, New York, New York 10014, USA

Penguin Group (Canada), 90 Eglinton Avenue East, Suite 700, Toronto, Ontario M4P 2Y3, Canada
(a division of Pearson Penguin Canada Inc.)
Penguin Books Ltd., 80 Strand, London WC2R 0RL, England
Penguin Group Ireland, 25 St. Stephen's Green, Dublin 2, Ireland (a division of Penguin Books Ltd.)
Penguin Group (Australia), 250 Camberwell Road, Camberwell, Victoria 3124, Australia
(a division of Pearson Australia Group Pty. Ltd.)
Penguin Books India Pvt. Ltd., 11 Community Centre, Panchsheel Park, New Delhi—110 017, India
Penguin Group (NZ), 67 Apollo Drive, Rosedale, North Shore 0632, New Zealand
(a division of Pearson New Zealand Ltd.)
Penguin Books (South Africa) (Pty.) Ltd., 24 Sturdee Avenue, Rosebank, Johannesburg 2196,
South Africa

Penguin Books Ltd., Registered Offices: 80 Strand, London WC2R 0RL, England

This is a work of fiction. Names, characters, places, and incidents either are the product of the author's imagination or are used fictitiously, and any resemblance to actual persons, living or dead, business establishments, events, or locales is entirely coincidental.

SLOCUM AND THE FOUR SEASONS

A Jove Book / published by arrangement with the author

PRINTING HISTORY
Jove edition / July 2010

Copyright © 2010 by Penguin Group (USA) Inc.
Cover illustration by Sergio Giovine.

ISBN: 978-0-515-14816-9

JOVE®
Jove Books are published by The Berkley Publishing Group,
a division of Penguin Group (USA) Inc.
375 Hudson Street, New York, New York 10014.
JOVE® is a registered trademark of Penguin Group (USA) Inc.
The "J" design is a trademark of Penguin Group (USA) Inc.

PRINTED IN THE UNITED STATES OF AMERICA

10 9 8 7 6 5 4 3 2 1

1

John Slocum had been hotter, thirstier, and more miserable in his day, but never had he seen such godforsaken land as Goose Flats. The alkali plain stretched all the way to the silver, mirage-shimmered horizon, and even the yucca and prickly pear cactus struggled to survive. The stunted creosote bushes barely exuded their characteristic odor because it took too much effort in the heat, and the occasional mesquite were testimony to water, but it was a long ways beneath the hooves of Slocum's mare. Too deep to mean squat to him or his horse.

Slocum kept his head down so the sweat would drip onto his saddle and not burn his eyes. His bandanna was pulled up over his nose to keep the choking dust from clogging his lungs, but worst of all was the way his mouth felt. If some small animal had crawled in there and died somewhere behind his molars, the foul taste couldn't be worse.

Slocum tried to remember when he had been comfortable. Benson? No, not there. The town marshal had taken a distinct dislike to him and run him out of town. Slocum wouldn't have stood for that kind of uncivil behavior except that the marshal had four brothers deputized to back his play, each bigger and meaner than the other. Sometimes, riding on was the smart thing to do, even if it meant getting lost, heading south a ways into the Sonoran Desert, and finally discovering the old road heading southeast toward Tombstone.

The twin ruts were permanent features of the dusty path. At one time rain had fallen, a wagon had driven by and cut grooves in the temporarily soft earth, then the sun had returned with a vengeance. No Indian pottery maker fired her pot hotter or harder than this ground. He stared, unseeing, at the ruts as his horse walked slowly, as tired and thirsty as he was. Squinting a little helped keep out the fierce sunlight, but nothing kept the gunshots from rumbling across the sun-hammered sand.

Looking up, Slocum got some stinging sweat into his eyes. He swiped it away as he slowly turned, focusing in on the distinctive sound of a rifle and possibly two pistols firing wildly. Good sense dictated that he ought to keep riding, or maybe find the dubious shade of a mesquite and wait for both the sun and the men spraying lead around so generously to go away.

That's what common sense told him to do. He urged his horse away from the rutted road in the direction of a low, sandy rise. As he worked his way up the slope, he saw the telltale S curves left in the sand by a sidewinder. When he reached the top of the dune, he saw another kind of sidewinder.

A quarter mile off, two men used a wagon as protection against three outlaws circling and shooting furiously at them. Whatever was in the wagon wasn't going anywhere. The outlaws had gunned down the horses. Even if the driver and the guard—that was the way Slocum read the drama playing out in front of him—survived the robbery and the less than accurate marksmanship of the road agents, they had a powerful long way to go before reaching Tombstone. Chances weren't too good any man on foot could walk a mile, much less all the way, across Goose Flats to what passed for a town.

Slocum pulled down his bandanna and wiped his dried lips. The guard wasn't going to have any trek facing him. A lucky shot from one outlaw had caught him in the face. Slocum watched as the man lifted his hands to his temples and then simply keeled over. He had died before he knew it.

"You won't get this shipment, you sons of bitches!" cried the driver. He grabbed up the guard's rifle and tried to lever in a round. The magazine was empty. He stepped away from the wagon and held the weapon like a baseball bat. The pitch sent by the closest robber wasn't going to be hit. It was a perfect strike in the driver's chest. Like his companion before, he sank to the ground and flopped back, faceup in the sun. It didn't matter one whit to him to sprawl out on burning sand. He was dead.

"This is it, men. We done struck it rich!"

The road agent who had gunned down the helpless driver yanked back a tarp and reached over into the wagon bed. His horse shied, but he viciously yanked at the reins to get back alongside the wagon.

"I swear, I never in all my born days saw a sight that purty," said another of the thieves. All three pulled down their masks, but Slocum was at too great a distance to get a good look at their faces. It wouldn't have mattered, even if he had been closer. They all stared at the cargo, faces away from him.

He considered slithering back down the sandy hill, retracing the sidewinder's path, finding those twin ruts, and continuing his dry, hot ride to Tombstone. He considered that. Then he decided he ought to cut himself in on some of that cargo. It didn't matter what had been in the wagon. Food? His belly growled. Water? He couldn't spit for the sand and tarry gunk in his mouth. And money? Not even two nickels to rub together rode in his vest pocket.

Whatever the road agents had found in the wagon would go a ways toward making life a damn sight more pleasant for John Slocum.

He rode down from the rise, to prevent them from spotting him outlined against the cloudless blue Arizona sky, and watched as they hovered like vultures around the wagon. They finally dismounted and began unloading what looked to be burlap bags. Slocum's heart raced. The wagon had been carrying a load of silver. The damn fool outlaws had killed the team hitched to the wagon or they could have made off with everything together. Instead, they divvied up the silver among themselves, causing their horses to protest when each was weighed down with two large, heavy bags.

Slocum considered his chances taking all three outlaws, then saw he wouldn't have that problem. Once they had transferred the load, they split up and rode in three different directions. When one headed straight for him, Slocum reached for the ebony handle of his Colt Navy slung in a cross-draw holster. He doubted the man could see him, not with the sun directly in his eyes. Before he had to draw and fire, Slocum watched the outlaw veer away and head southwest. Slocum waited until he disappeared down an arroyo before walking his horse toward the now quiet wagon.

His horse tried to bolt when she smelled the spilled blood. Buzzards circling above spiraled downward for their afternoon meal, but Slocum's presence denied them their repast. For the moment.

Slocum made certain the guard and driver were dead. Even from a distance, his appraisal of the killing shots had been fairly accurate. The guard had a bullet in one side of his head and not much in the way of a skull left on the other, and the driver had been plugged square in the heart. The horses were already drawing flies and ants; it took all of Slocum's skill to keep his own mount under control at the stench of rapidly decaying horseflesh.

He rode to the rear of the wagon and saw some supplies.

He helped himself to the flour and jerky and, even better, to a large container of water. It sloshed about as he drank. Then he wrenched off the top and put it on the ground. It wasn't much for the mare, but it was better than nothing. If the horse died, so did he. The sun sinking lower in the west, over the distant Whitestone Mountains did nothing to alleviate thirst. If anything, it seemed hotter now than at high noon.

"Drink up, what there is," Slocum said, patting the horse's neck. The water provided only a couple gulps for the thirsty animal, but it would have to do. They had a trail to follow.

Slocum circled the wagon, looking at the faint impressions in the thin layer of dust on the ground. The outlaws riding to the north and northeast would be harder to follow than the third who had ridden toward the sun. The setting sun would highlight his tracks and cast faint shadows toward Slocum as he rode. It wasn't much, but it would have to do.

He checked the wagon bed one last time. Nothing. The six bags of silver had been the sole cargo. He couldn't get all six, but a pair of those heavy bags would satisfy him.

Slocum started riding. He lost the trail now and then, but as the sun sank lower, it made the hoofprints more visible, until the sun vanished entirely. The outlaw had not bothered hiding his trail and had gone straight toward Fort Huachuca. Slocum doubted that was his destination. More likely, he intended on crossing the border from Arizona Territory into Mexico, where he could live like a king on that much silver.

"Uneasy lies the crowned head," Slocum said. The heat from the day had turned icy cold in less than a half hour—and this betrayed his quarry. The man had camped, starting a blazing fire for cooking and warmth. Slocum spotted it from a half mile off.

The lazy spiral of wood smoke carried the scent of fresh meat cooking. Slocum relished the way his mouth watered at the promise of food—and the moisture it brought to his bone-dry tongue. The still night would cloak him if he waited for complete darkness. The urge to simply ride into the outlaw's camp and gun him down was great, but Slocum couldn't forget the other two outlaws and how they had ridden off with a fortune in silver. If he managed to recover a third of the silver shipment, why not all of it? After all, it wasn't as if he was stealing from the company shipping the precious metal. He was only taking what had been took already.

He dismounted. His horse let out a gusty sigh of relief that worried him. The sound carried in the rapidly cooling air. He drew his six-shooter and advanced cautiously. When he reached a spot near the campsite, he sank to the ground and flopped on his belly to scout.

Bulling his way into the camp would have been disastrous. As his eyes adjusted to the combination of twilight and dancing flame from the fire, he came to the uneasy realization that the outlaw wasn't in camp. His horse had been hobbled a few yards away and valiantly nibbled at desiccated mesquite pods. Slocum strained to hear since vision wasn't giving him what he needed.

The cooking meat was burning now. The outlaw had bagged a rabbit and skewered it to roast over the fire. Thick, greasy clouds rose skyward, obscuring the first stars of the evening. Slocum clutched his pistol a little tighter. He made out the dim shapes of the robber's gear. The bedroll, saddle, and rifle were to one side of the fire. But nowhere did he see the outlaw or the twin bags of silver.

Lack of food and water made his mind drift. Was he going to steal silver coins or ingots? It didn't matter. He might even get silver shavings. That would be good, almost as good as gold dust.

The visions of wealth dancing in his head almost betrayed him. From his left he heard the soft crunch of boots grinding down into the dried ground. He rolled on this side and thrust his Colt Navy out, but he didn't cock it. The sound would have been as startling in the still night as if he had fired a round.

The outlaw huffed and puffed and passed within yards of Slocum, never knowing he was being watched.

When he saw his dinner was burning, he cursed a blue streak and grabbed for the stick, yanking it away from the flames. He swung the burned rabbit about in the air and got the flames out. He sat and whipped out a knife to saw off pieces of the tough, charred meat.

Slocum rolled back onto his belly and aimed his six-shooter, but he hesitated in cutting the unaware man down, because of what he was doing. The man gnawed on a piece of meat and balanced a sheet of paper on his knee. Juggling paper, rabbit, and the stub of a pencil, he worked to write something on the paper.

Slocum rose to his knees to get a better look at the camp. If he had to, he could fire in a split second, but he wanted to know where the silver was before making a move.

No silver.

Then Slocum saw that the man had gone off and returned with a short-handled shovel. Moving slowly, Slocum settled back to the ground and studied the outlaw closely. The man looked up now and again, getting his bearings from the stars, then checking the position of the distant mountains. Slocum could come to only one conclusion. The man had buried the silver and now drew himself a map so he could find it again.

A slow smile crossed Slocum's lips. A different plan formed, one that he liked more than just gunning down the man who had cold-bloodedly murdered the driver and wagon guard. It required all the willpower he could muster to simply lie on his belly, watching the outlaw until he tucked away his treasure map, spread his blanket, and went to sleep. Slocum gave him a full half hour to get into a deep sleep before moving as quietly as any Chiricahua Apache roaming this desert.

The outlaw's horse nickered as Slocum approached, then the animal fell silent. Slocum reached the outlaw's side and kept his six-gun pointed at the man's head as he deftly reached into his pocket and drew out the treasure map. When he had it free of the man's vest pocket, Slocum picked up the shovel and backed from camp, until he reached a spot where he could unfold the map and study it.

Knowing the direction the man had come from after burying the silver let Slocum orient himself quickly. The map was a crude one, more a memory jogger than a real map for someone else to follow. This made Slocum even more ebullient. He held up the map, then began walking. He almost tripped as his toe slipped into softer earth.

The outlaw had buried the silver in the center of a ring of greasewood and mesquite bushes for easier locating. Slocum dropped to his knees and began digging like a prairie dog. It took less than a minute to unearth the two bags of silver coins. He ran his fingers over the first thick canvas bag and around the outlines of the coins poking from the inside. When he realized his fingers were beginning to bleed on the canvas, he stopped. It took another few minutes to scrape the dirt back into the hole so it mounded up the way it had after the outlaw finished his initial burial.

Slocum lugged the bags of coins to where he had left his horse. He started to strap them on, then decided to let his horse rest a little longer before adding a full fifty-pound additional burden to her back.

The mare whinnied, as if thanking him, but Slocum knew the horse would soon be cursing him in whatever equine language she spoke. He patted the mare's neck, then hurried back to the campsite. He approached with less stealth this time because he heard the outlaw's loud snores.

Putting the folded map back into the man's vest pocket proved a little more difficult than he'd expected, but Slocum succeeded without waking him. He put the shovel back where he had found it, then stopped and stared. The canteen beckoned. It was foolish, but Slocum couldn't stop himself. He uncorked the canteen and drank. He had intended to take only a sip, but the tepid water tasted better than any whiskey he had ever thrown down his gullet. When the canteen was almost drained, he stopped.

The outlaw would know something was amiss when he found he was almost out of water.

A sudden inspiration struck Slocum. He finished the water, letting some of it slosh over his face and hands. A small night breeze had kicked up. The evaporation on his face felt frigid and invigorating. Carefully staging his drama, Slocum pushed the cork almost all the way back in, then laid the canteen down in such a way that it might have tipped over. With the cork not secure, the contents could have leaked into the thirsty desert. Only then did he slowly, quietly depart.

When he got back to his mare, he found that he was right about her balking under the load of silver and his own weight. Somehow, whether it was the water or the prospect of being rich, Slocum found it easier to sling the heavy silver onto the horse and walk through the increasingly chilly night.

When the outlaw returned to claim his loot, he would never find the right spot. Ever. The joke would be on the thief, and Slocum could savor it for years, imagining the man's growing frustration as he tried to follow his map to the treasure.

This was worth being run out of Benson.

2

The nearer Slocum got to Tombstone, the edgier he grew. The last thing he wanted to do was ride into a boomtown with two huge bags filled with silver coins. Even if the marshal didn't think he had stolen them from the shipment and was responsible for the deaths of two men, the attention this would generate would be enough for him to get shot in the back the first time he looked in the wrong direction.

Considering the heft of the coins, he approached the town from the south. Goose Flats didn't afford many hiding places, but he knew he could find a spot easily remembered. Unlike the outlaw from whom he had stolen the silver, he wouldn't need a map to find it again. A couple miles outside town, he located the perfect spot. Far to the east rose a pair of distinctive peaks and a desolate patch of ground was filled with curiously shaped holes that looked as if some rock-eating monster had burrowed down hunting for prey. He unloaded the silver from the mare, much to the horse's relief. Slocum dragged the bags to a hole, got a decent idea how to mark it with three stone cairns some distance away, then covered the bags after taking a handful of coins.

He held one up and studied it closely. It wasn't as much a coin as it was a silver slug. It lacked the usual design stamped into it, and the edges had not been milled to prevent anyone from shaving off some of the precious metal and still spending the coin. Slocum shrugged it off. It was silver. He could tell by running his fingers across the surface. Like gold, silver had its own feel.

This was what it felt like to be rich. If he found the other two road agents, he would be really rich.

After tromping down the dirt on top of his loot, he stepped back and thought hard about the robbery. Why had the outlaw decided to bury his share? Then Slocum laughed. The outlaw had buried the stolen silver for the same reason he just had. To waltz into a town—maybe Fort Huachuca—with that much silver would draw unwanted attention. At the fort, arousing the curiosity of the cavalry was even less a good thing. For all the outlaw knew, the post commander might actually believe that laws ought to be enforced, and no drifter was likely to have come by fifty pounds of unminted silver coins honestly.

It took Slocum the better part of two hours to travel the two miles into Tombstone. The approach from the south was rugged and steep. The only saving grace he saw was that Tombstone was situated above the dreary flatness of Goose Flats.

Before he reached Allen Street, filled with side-by-side saloons, he saw why Tombstone was such a boomtown. Businesses selling every imaginable type of mining equipment were jammed with eager customers. From their look, they ranged from hard rock miners to prospectors to gents in fancy duds who probably owned working silver mines. Slocum touched one of the silver slugs in his vest pocket and wondered whose metal he carried. From the attack out in the desert, it wasn't possible to tell if the wagon had been coming or going. There was little reason to believe anyone brought silver to Tombstone. It must have been a shipment away from town, possibly intended for transport on a train to points east or maybe out to the mint in San Francisco for stamping and milling.

He shrugged it off. What did it matter? There wasn't any way to tell which mine the silver had come from, but if he listened hard enough, he was likely to find out who had made a recent shipment. The original owner of the silver slugs, however, mattered less to him than the current owner.

And the current owner intended to fill his gut with food and beer.

Slocum dismounted and went into the nearest saloon. A wave of cigar smoke and body heat boiled out from inside as he stood in the door. He sucked in a lungful of the foul air and relished it. The long bar to his right stretched all the way to the rear of the narrow room. Mirrors reflected the light seeping in from outside and magnified it until anyone could have read a newspaper without an effort. But nobody inside was reading. A half dozen miners pressed close to the bar, beers in front of them. A dozen tables along the left wall marched like soldiers on a parade ground to a rear door. A crude painting of a naked reclining woman was proudly displayed behind the barkeep, who worked his crowd quickly and efficiently.

Before Slocum stepped inside, the barkeep called out, "Beer, mister? Got some iced down just for you."

"And a sandwich to go with it. What do you have?"

"Roast beef. A pickle. The lot is yours for a dime."

"Sold," Slocum said. He hesitantly pulled a silver slug from his pocket. Would flashing this brand him as a robber or was it simply the currency for a mining town? He would find out. He dropped it on the bar, letting it sing out its silver song until it lay flat.

The barkeep snatched it before Slocum could square himself against the bar.

"Here you go," the barkeep said, dropping a frosty beer mug and a plate with the sandwich and a pickle in front of

Slocum. He dropped a handful of coins and a couple sheets
of scrip as change. Slocum didn't bother asking how the
barkeep had determined how much metal was in the slug.
It didn't pay to question too much until he found out how
things worked in town. Chances were good he had just been
cheated, but the sight of food and beer took away any sting.

Slocum had drifted through the West long enough to
know small towns shared traits, but there were always some
small details that distinguished one from another. Mining
towns tended to be lawless, no matter the number of mar-
shals and deputies patrolling the streets. But there was always
a single man whose word was gospel. Determining who this
was and steering clear of him was the best way to leave town
on horseback rather than staying in the town cemetery.

Listening to the others along the bar gave Slocum a better idea of Tombstone and how it worked. There were several large silver mines, a couple big producing ones that ran
a hundred feet under the streets of the town itself. No matter where color showed in rock, men would dig for it. It
surprised Slocum that there weren't any poker games in the
saloon. Nor did he see any soiled doves.

"Business so good you don't need gambling or women?"
Slocum asked the barkeep when he came back with a second beer.

"Just got to town. This here saloon's been open almost a
day. I need to recruit some tinhorns and ladies." He eyed
Slocum. "You don't have the look of a gambler." He paused
and then asked, "When I get the ladies working, you interested in being a bouncer?"

Slocum said nothing as he studied the barkeep. The man
was burly enough to act as his own bouncer, but Slocum
saw the glint in his left eye. Glass. There was a curious way
he put the beer on the bar. A poorly mended right arm. He
limped a mite, too, as he went from one end of the bar to
the other.

"You want my gun?"

"As long as it's slung on your hip, yeah," the barkeep answered honestly. "I've owned gin mills in a dozen different towns and the one thing that never changes is a drunk miner or cowboy or soldier wanting to blow off steam. I don't mind 'em pounding on each other, but when it comes to shooting up the place, I draw the line."

"Don't know if I want to stay or keep riding," Slocum answered.

"You hang around Tombstone, you got a job. I like your looks."

"Enough to give me a free beer?"

"I don't like my own mama's looks enough for that." The barkeep laughed and moved to grab a dime off the bar and pour another shot of whiskey for the man next to Slocum.

Slocum nursed his beer, enjoying the cool liquid slipping down his gullet. He shook his head, considering how his luck had changed so fast. After being run out of Benson, he'd thought nothing could be worse than struggling across the Sonoran Desert in the middle of summer, broke and damned near dead from lack of water. Then he had seen two men whose fortune had turned even worse than his, and somehow everything had started coming up roses for him.

The two bags of silver buried out in the desert would keep him in fine steak dinners and beer for a long time, and he had hardly been in town a half hour when he'd been offered a job that didn't require him burrowing underground like a mole, only seeing the light of day by accident and living with the constant fear of a cave-in. If it hadn't been for the silver he had stolen from a murderer and thief, he would have jumped at the chance of working here.

He looked around. For a saloon that had opened only a few hours back, it had a certain elegance to it lacking in most boomtown watering holes. He had passed the Crystal Palace and heard the bawdy songs coming from inside, the laughter and the occasional angry voice, but that place had none of the curious charm this one did.

Slocum almost called the owner back to take the job.

A scuffle outside stopped him. He turned, braced his elbows against the bar, and stared outside. The bright sunlight made him squint, then his eyes opened on their own to take in the woman's shapely figure and delightful profile. She had a sharp chin that jutted out belligerently, and the set to her shoulders told of a strong woman who was pissed off. Long waterfalls of auburn hair cascaded down to her shoulders. As she shook her head from side to side, it flowed away and formed a mist that almost hid her face.

For a brief instant Slocum got a clear look at her face. He had seen beautiful women in his day, but this one led the parade. Were her eyes bright green to match his own or were they bluer than the summer Arizona sky? It was a question he wouldn't mind getting a firsthand answer to.

Then he lost any chance of finding out this important detail. A tall man, whipcord thin and taller than Slocum's six-feet-plus, stepped forward and swung. His fist connected with the woman's chin, snapping her head back. She sank straight to the boardwalk, obviously unconscious.

Slocum didn't even remember crossing the barroom floor and stepping outside. His fist traveled only a few inches but sank up to the wrist in the man's belly. For an instant the shock from the impact echoed all the way up to Slocum's shoulder and jarred him. He might have tried to punch through a brick wall. Then he felt the heavily muscled slab of gut yield and the man doubled over. Air gushed form his lungs and he stumbled, reaching down with one hand to keep from tumbling into the street.

"Get up," Slocum said. "I want to hit you again."

The man gasped for air. His hatchet-thin face turned up to Slocum's. Slocum had wondered if the woman had blue eyes. This man's eyes were so blue they might have been chips of ice. Under the tan beaten into his face by wind and sun shimmered a curious paleness.

"Who are you?"

"The man who is going to whup up on you." Slocum reckoned that if the man had enough breath to ask questions, he was strong enough to fight. He swung and narrowly missed the man's chin for a blow matching the one delivered to the woman. Slocum's fist slid along one leather-tough cheek and sent the man staggering, but he came to his feet out in the street. He reached up and touched the shallow cut Slocum had opened on his face.

"I'm bleedin'."

"Not enough." Slocum went after him, but the man backpedaled and forced Slocum to slow his attack. If he rushed in pell-mell, he was likely to make a mistake. The man had the look of a pure killer. Any misstep now might be Slocum's last. He had started the fight, and he intended to finish it.

"You don't know who I am?"

"Don't care." Slocum moved in such a way that he presented his left shoulder to the man. He could whip out his six-shooter from the cross-draw holster and move only a few inches to bring the owlhoot into his sights.

"I'm Win Winthrop," the man said. "Ain't no man gets by hittin' on me like you just did."

"Do something about it? Or do you only beat up women?"

For a moment, Winthrop looked confused. Then he laughed harshly.

"Her? This is all about her? She got you wrapped round her little finger like she has most of the men in this godforsaken hellhole?"

"Shit or get off the pot," Slocum said.

"You want me to go for my gun, don't you?"

Slocum said nothing. A coldness draped him now and turned him into an emotionless killer. His hands were steady and his breathing slow and regular. All he needed was to see the slightest twitch in Winthrop's hand and he would go for his six-gun.

"You're a gunfighter. And . . . and my hand's hurt."

"Hitting a woman in the face will do that," Slocum said.

"Wait, don't." The voice came from behind, but Slocum didn't turn to see who spoke. The instant his attention strayed, Winthrop would go for his hogleg.

The woman brushed past him and stood between them, her back to Slocum. She stamped her foot and put her balled hands on her ample hips.

"How dare you strike me, Win! You never knew how to treat a woman."

"Get out of the way, Spring. I got a man to kill. Then we'll finish our business."

Slocum drew, cocked his Colt Navy, and had it aimed straight at Winthrop's head even as he pushed the woman to one side. She stumbled and went to hands and knees in the street. Slocum froze Winthrop with his hand halfway to his pistol.

"Don't, mister. I'm backin' off." Winthrop moved his hands away from his body and held them level with his shoulders on either side of his body.

"Apologize."

"I've got nuthin' to apologize to you for!"

The way the man's anger flared, Slocum thought he would finally have his chance to cut him down as he went for his six-shooter. But Winthrop got his temper under control before he made the move that would have sent him out to Boot Hill.

When he saw that Winthrop wasn't going to draw, Slocum explained. "To her. Apologize to the lady."

"Lady? She's no lady. She's only a cheap—" Winthrop saw what his reward would be if he continued his tirade.

"Spring, I'm sorry," he said insincerely.

"Go to hell, Win. You're going to pay for this. Give me that gun, mister, and I'll do what you won't!"

The auburn-haired woman grabbed for Slocum's six-gun, but he moved at the last instant and she missed, stumbling between the men again. This was all it took for Winthrop to hightail it. He turned and ran, spurs tinkling like silver bells as he ducked down an alley, heading toward Fremont Street.

"You should have killed him. He's a dangerous man."

"You're welcome," Slocum said, slipping his six-shooter back into his holster. Winthrop might stop running by the time he reached the far side of Goose Flats—or maybe he'd keep riding. Slocum hoped the Apaches caught him and worked their particular greeting on him. Winthrop might last as long as a day.

"What?"

"You have men beat you up like that often?" Slocum studied the woman's lovely face for signs of bruises or cuts. Other than a growing bruise on her chin, her complexion was flawless. He frowned a little as he continued studying her. She looked like someone he knew, but he couldn't place her.

"Of course not. Quite the contrary, usually," she said, favoring him with a smile as bright as the sun beating down on Tombstone.

Slocum waited for something more from her, but it never came. He wasn't sure what he expected, but gratitude wasn't part of the package.

"Obliged to have been of service," Slocum said, touching the brim of his hat. Another beer would go a ways toward getting the bad taste out of his mouth.

He had reached the saloon door when she called, "I never got your name."

"No, you didn't," Slocum said. The beer already sitting on the bar beckoned, the barkeep watching him like a hawk. Slocum's thirst grew by the second.

"I'm Spring Atkins."

"Pleased to make your acquaintance, ma'am," Slocum said. He turned from the auburn-haired beauty out in the middle of Allen Street and went into the saloon. The heat was different inside, but the beer washed away all his concerns.

3

"That was smart," the barkeep said, pushing another beer in front of Slocum.

"What do you mean?" Slocum looked up into the man's sharp eye. Somehow, he found the glass eye distracting. One-eyed or not, he got the feeling not much got past the bar owner.

"Walking away from her. She's a looker, no doubt about that, but she's pure poison."

"I couldn't let her get beat up. Not by an owlhoot like that."

"Winthrop is a dangerous cayuse. I ran into him a couple weeks back over in Fairbank. Watch your back. He's more likely to send a bullet to your spine than to face you down."

"I got that," he said. Slocum ran his hand up and down the side of the beer mug. The coolness told him the barkeep spent a great deal of money shipping ice in from higher altitudes. The price of the beer was worth the chill against his hand after pulling leather for so long across the desert.

The barkeep hesitated, looked at customers at the far end who were banging shot glasses against the bar to get his attention. Whiskey needed pouring, but he didn't move.

"The job's still yours, if you'll take it. I liked the way you handled yourself."

"You wouldn't want to hire me. Winthrop might gun me down on the premises," Slocum said. To his surprise, the barkeep laughed and went to serve up the liquor.

Slocum twisted to the side and was reaching for his Colt Navy when a hand lightly descended on his shoulder.

"My, you're as jumpy as a long-tailed cat laying next to a rocking chair," Spring Atkins said.

"You shouldn't be in here," Slocum said, startled anew at seeing that it was her hand on his shoulder.

"I wanted to talk to you, and waiting outside in the sun didn't suit me. The way you're making love to that old beer told me you're likely to be here a long time."

"You think so?"

"I suspect you'd take a long time with any lovemaking," she said boldly.

"Let's step outside."

"Your concern over my reputation is touching," Spring said. "I will be happy to accompany you outside." She took his arm and steered him toward the door. Slocum found himself tensing because he knew every eye in the saloon was on his back, and he knew what they were all thinking about Spring Atkins. For all he knew, they might be right.

When they got outside, he felt sweat beading on his forehead and wasn't sure it came entirely from the heat. Spring turned and pressed close to him, her breasts brushing across his chest and her face only inches from his.

"We got off to a bad start. I am grateful for what you did to send Win on his way."

"How do you know him?"

Spring looked away and shook her head. A rueful smile danced on her full red lips.

"There are some things in a woman's life she simply cannot avoid. Win is one of those."

"He ever hit you before?" Slocum watched her face carefully but could not tell if she was lying when she said that he hadn't. "You might leave town—and him—behind."

"I can't do that," she said. "And you shouldn't believe every rumor you hear." Her eyes darted in the direction of the saloon and those standing there, still intently watching. "Well, it depends on the rumor." She smiled winningly.

"Why can't you leave? Your husband won't let you?"

Her face melted and her lips thinned to a razor's slash.

"He's dead, for all I care."

"Sorry," Slocum said.

"He's no more than a memory for me."

"You seem to attract the wrong kind of man."

"Do I now?" Spring moved closer and reached out to lightly put her hand on his shoulder. "Are you the right kind of man?"

"No."

"Then you can help me again," she said. Her body swayed slightly, sinuously rubbing against him like a cat. "I need someone who knows mining."

"I've been a miner and don't like it. The desert sun might be burning my skin, but that's better than never seeing the sun at all."

"But you do know your way around a mine. You can help me with advice. I own the Silver Chalice out east of town. It might be the richest mine in all of Arizona Territory."

"You don't need me then," Slocum said, but he was intrigued in spite of himself. Beautiful, young, and rich, Spring Atkins was enough of a mystery to beguile him with her ways. He knew how his curiosity got him into trouble time and time again, but there was nowhere he had to be, and two big bags of silver buried south of town made him the equal of any mine owner. A lovely woman completed the picture for him of how to spend some time. She certainly acted as if she was willing to help him find ways of whiling away the hours. For a day or two, at least.

"I have a miner working the claim, but he seems so . . ."

"Inept?"

"Drunk. All the time," she said. "I worry that he might hurt himself. If you could come to the Silver Chalice and give him some advice about mining and safety, I'd be ever so grateful."

Everything in Slocum's head screamed, *Gallop in the opposite direction*, but he said, "Where's this Silver Chalice?"

Her smile widened even more, showing straight white teeth. Spring Atkins was a woman blessed by nature.

"Follow me. My buckboard's around back. It's several miles, but we can reach the mine before sundown." She looked boldly at him.

"Reckon that'd mean I'd have to spend the night. Is there somewhere I can spread my bedroll?"

"I'm sure there will be." Spring turned, brushed against him provocatively, and walked away, just enough hitch in her git along to let him know what would be spread once he got to the silver mine.

Slocum knew he ought to go back into the saloon and have another beer. He knew a lot of things. He stepped up onto his horse and headed eastward, spotting Spring in her buckboard within a few minutes. Trotting to narrow the gap between them, he finally rode alongside her. The noise and dust made conversation difficult since she set such a spirited pace, but Slocum didn't mind. He was too busy thinking about what was going to happen once they reached the mine.

A little before sundown, Spring took a turnoff and drove another mile into the hills. Slocum was a little surprised to see a miner sitting on a rusted ore cart, building himself a smoke. The miner glanced up, a sour look on his face, then called out, "Welcome back, Miz Atkins."

"How's it gone today, Jerome?"

The miner shrugged.

Spring turned to Slocum and gave him a look that said, "See what I mean?"

Slocum dismounted and went to a small mountain of ore that had been pulled from the Silver Chalice. The mouth of the mine loomed dark and ominous, with just a hint of blasting powder lingering in the air. Jerome had blasted today.

"You pulled a fair amount of ore, if you blasted this morning."

"Afternoon," Jerome said, puffing on his cigarette.

"You're working hard," Slocum said.

Jerome's eyebrows arched. He looked more attentively at Slocum. "Yeah" was all he said.

"Come to the house," Spring said. "I'm famished."

"Yeah, go heat up a can of beans," Jerome said.

Slocum ignored the jibe and followed Spring to a small house, hardly more than a line shack. She secured the horse's reins to a post but left it hitched to the buckboard.

"I'll tend to the horse later," she said, seeing his expression. "And you can tend to yours. Afterward."

He took the time to unsaddle his horse and lead it to a water barrel. He patted the horse as he looked around for some feed.

"Soup's on," Spring called, standing in the doorway. She leaned against the frame, but Slocum noticed right away she had unbuttoned her blouse down to a point halfway between her jutting breasts. "You don't mind that I'm not a good cook? Jerome was right about that."

"There are other talents," Slocum said. She didn't move from the narrow doorway, making him press against her to get inside. The cabin was dominated by a large bed and a Franklin stove. A small table had been pushed against the far wall under a window. The glass pane had cracked and was too dirty to see through.

"Make yourself comfortable," Spring said. "I am."

He turned and saw how accurate that was. She shucked off her blouse and stood naked to the waist. She tossed the garment onto the lone chair in the room and stood with her hands on her hips.

"Your turn."

Slocum smiled. He discarded his gunbelt, added his Stetson, coat, and vest, then began working on his shirt. He wasn't working fast enough for the woman. Spring took two quick steps and stopped in front of him. Her lips parted slightly and her eyelids drooped to half-mast. As he bent to kiss her, he found himself missing his target. She dropped to her knees in front of him and eagerly worked on the buttons holding his fly shut.

"Yes," she said, finding his hidden treasure. Slocum groaned as she pulled his manhood out and her mouth engulfed the bulbous tip. He stiffened quickly as her lips and tongue worked all over him. He reached down and laid his hands on her head. He felt the life within this woman, her vibrancy and ardor as she worked back and forth on his length. Slocum sighed as she slipped closer and closer to his groin, taking him fully. Then she pulled back and looked up, her blue eyes bright with lust.

"Your turn," she said.

Slocum knew what she wanted and was willing to give it to her. He kicked free of his boots and pulled his jeans off while she watched. Then he went to her and placed his palms against her breasts. The sleek flow of her tender flesh excited him, and his touch did even more for Spring. She shivered in delight as he pressed down firmly and then cupped those finely shaped breasts, getting her up to her feet.

"I want you to—"

He cut off her demand with his lips. He kissed her fully and deeply. Their tongues dueled back and forth, playing an erotic game of hide-and-seek while he reached behind her and ran his hands down over her naked back and moved lower until he cupped her ass. He squeezed. She moaned and pressed even closer to him, her naked breasts crushing into his bare chest. He felt her nipples harden with need as he continued to massage.

Then he found the hooks and released her skirt. She

kicked free so they were both naked and pressing hotly into each other.

Slocum felt their sweat mingle. They began moving against each other, slipping easily because of the moisture.

Turning around and around, Slocum maneuvered her to the bed. She sat and he followed her down and kept slipping until he knelt on the floor. An auburn thatch just inches from his face was already dotted with her inner juices. He lapped at them. Spring gasped and leaned back. She lifted her feet to the edge of the bed and spread her legs wide so he could burrow his face downward.

He lapped at her and dipped his tongue into her well, causing her to shudder all over.

"Oh, yes, yes, so nice. Your mouth. Just what I—" She cried out as he began moving his tongue in and out of her with as much speed as he could. He slithered about her pink nether lips and then turned to kiss her inner thighs.

Slocum was suddenly deaf and blind when she clamped her thighs down on either side of his head.

He waited for the spasm to pass and then worked farther up, above the fleecy triangle nestled between her legs to her belly and even higher, until he kissed and licked between her breasts. She took his head in her hands and kept him firmly at the spot where she wanted the most attention.

Slocum kept moving and felt her entire body shake like a leaf in a high wind as he slipped his manhood far into her. For a moment he simply stopped and relished the sensations building within him. Her tight, hot female sheath clamped down all around his hidden length until he was certain he couldn't take any more. The moment passed. He slipped back slowly.

"Oh, you know how to torment me. I . . . I can't stand any more. I can't!"

Slocum wasn't going to be rushed. He got her off again with his methodical moves, his deep thrusts followed by a long, lingering moment before retreating. She clawed at his arms as he supported himself above her. Spring's face was a mask of pure desire. She tossed her head from side to side as her desires reached the breaking point.

As she exploded, her legs wrapped around his waist and pulled him even deeper, her ankles locked behind his back. She clawed at his arms and lifted herself up, arching to get even more of his shaft. Slocum wanted this to last forever. She was a beautiful woman and obviously lusty. She knew the right things to do, to touch, to squeeze and lick and even scratch. But he wasn't able to prolong this moment any longer.

He sank deeper into her sweet core, and then the heat in his fleshy boiler was not to be denied. He felt as if he was being crushed from all directions. The heat mounted until he was boiling inside. The tide rose, and no matter how he tried he could not prolong it. He exploded as he felt the woman thrashing beneath him. She cried out in passion and tried to squeeze the life out of him.

Slocum sank down and pressed her into the hard bed. Spring gasped for breath and only slowly regained her senses. Her eyes blinked and finally focused on him.

"You're really something special. I'm glad you rode into my life," she said.

"I don't have any complaints, either. Not after that," he said.

"The best you ever had, right?" she said. She pushed him to one side. Slocum felt their skin peeling apart. They had sweat even more, until they were almost glued together. The faint breeze coming through the cabin wall as the evening wind rose outside cooled him. Chilled him.

Spring reached over and batted his limp organ about.

"All gone."

"It can come back, but it needs to rest awhile." Slocum needed to rest, too. He had been in the saddle for long days and had committed a robbery and now this bout with Spring had taken it out of him.

"I've got a question," she said.

"What?"

"I didn't catch your name."

Slocum was dumbstruck for a moment, then realized he had never told her. He did now.

"You're a great catch, John Slocum," she declared.

"You always go to bed with men when you don't even know their names?" he had to ask.

She shrugged delightfully, causing her breasts to shimmy about just the right amount.

"I'm adaptable. Living in this godforsaken place makes a woman adaptable."

"So it seems. I like your adaptation," he said, fingering one pink nipple. As he toyed with it, he felt her heart beginning to beat faster. The tiny nub hardened. He knew she would be ready long before he was, but he could keep her occupied in other ways. As he reached down between her legs, his finger questing for the moist cranny there, he stopped.

"Keep going," she urged. "I want—"

"Quiet," he said sharply. He sat up, batted her hand away as she reached for him, and then he quickly stood. Slocum moved to the door and opened it a few inches. He caught a gust of dust-laden wind in the face, but along with that came another scent that bothered him.

"Did you hear a gunshot?"

"Why? Was that the sound I made when I got off?" She lounged on the bed on her side, propping her head up on her hand. "It felt as if I'd been shot. Hot, sharp, utterly indescribable." She sat up and frowned. "What do you think you're doing, John?"

He didn't answer as he pulled on his jeans. Getting into his boots took longer, but he didn't want to walk around the Silver Chalice barefoot. There must be a ton of sharp-edged stones pulled out of the mine. He would have bloodied feet in a few steps without the boots. But he didn't bother with his shirt, vest, and coat. He grabbed his Colt Navy and went back to the door.

"If you don't want to have me again, just say so," Spring said.

"There's someone out there," Slocum said.

"Of course there is. Jerome has a lean-to next to the mouth of the mine."

As he held the door against the wind, another shot rang out. It sounded different to him from the first shot.

"At least two guns are being fired."

"You're jumping to conclusions, John. Really. Come back and—"

Her words were cut off by a volley that made it sound as if Antietam were being fought all over again. Echoes and new reports became deafening.

"Stay here." He turned and looked at her flopped naked on the bed. "You might want to get dressed."

"Oh, I'm sure you can handle it. Hurry back. This will be waiting for you." Spring rolled onto her back, lifted her knees and wantonly exposed herself. Then she laughed as Slocum stepped outside. He pulled the door shut behind him. He made sure the latch was secure before looking around for some high ground where he could scout what was happening. To blunder into the middle of a gunfight was a sure way of getting ventilated.

He moved slowly toward a pile of dross, circled it, and then carefully climbed to the top, about ten feet above ground level. The edges of the rock cut at his hands and knees as he scrambled up, but when he reached the summit, he was glad he had chosen to be so cautious.

More gunshots rang out. In the night he saw three orange tongues of flame. He couldn't tell if one man had fired three times as he ran toward the mine or if three gunmen had each fired once. It didn't matter since the focus of all that firepower centered on the mine.

Slocum blinked as a shotgun fired. He was staring directly at the mine shaft when the night filled with the muzzle flash from the double-barreled flesh shredder. The flash dazzled him. He heard one more shot from what he took to be a six-shooter and then there was silence. Deathly silence.

The dancing spots faded from his vision. Slocum made his way down the back side of the pile of drossy rock and then warily moved toward the Silver Chalice. Only silence met him as he approached the mouth of the mine.

He went into a crouch, six-gun thrust out in front of him, when he saw a pair of boots sticking out of the mine. Advancing slowly, he made out the legs and the body and finally Jerome's dead body. He had caught a slug in the middle of his chest. A shotgun lay beside him. Slocum picked it up and broke it open to see that it held two fired shells.

"I hope you got a piece of him," Slocum said to the corpse, putting the shotgun back on the ground.

He pressed his bare back against the cold rock of the hillside and began moving in the direction that had to have been taken by Jerome's killer. A sudden click of rock against rock alerted him.

Slocum spun, cocked his six-shooter, and froze. His finger had started back on the trigger when he saw a ghostly white figure coming toward him.

"What's going on, John?" Spring called. She hadn't bothered to put on any clothes other than her shoes. As fetching as it was seeing such a naked vision of beauty, Slocum snapped at her.

"Get down. Somebody's killed Jerome."

"Oh, really. That's ridiculous. Who'd— Oh my god, no!" She let out a shriek that could have been heard all the way back in Tombstone.

Slocum went to her and clamped his hand over her mouth.

"The killer's still out there." He tightened his grip on her as she began struggling. He had no other choice but to keep her quiet or she was going to put them both in jeopardy.

Jerome had fought, and it hadn't done him any good. Slocum wasn't going to die as easily—and he wasn't about to let the naked Spring Atkins die that way, either.

4

"He's dead," Spring Atkins said in a voice so low Slocum could hardly hear her over the rising wind. "Who killed him?"

"I don't know," Slocum said, "because I couldn't get a good look during the gunfight. He might have hit his attacker." Slocum knelt and dragged his fingers through the dry dust till he touched a wet spot. In the moonlight the tip of his finger showed an inky blackness. He had seen blood by moonlight enough times to recognize it. Even if it hadn't been wet in a hard desert, he would have figured Jerome had winged his attacker. It was hard to miss even a moving target with a double-barreled shotgun.

"They were coming after me," Spring said. "Jerome gave his life defending me."

Slocum saw no reason to believe that. Jerome probably had enemies of his own. He might have insulted a miner in town and paid the price for it. Perhaps he owed money and his "banker" had finally collected the debt. Having met Jerome for only a few minutes, Slocum couldn't say about his personality, but it had seemed prickly. It wouldn't take much for him to rub a man the wrong way. Whether that had happened was a question Slocum couldn't answer.

"Noble of him to die that way, if they were coming for you," Slocum said. He looked up at the woman. Her naked body trembled from the cold wind whistling past the mine. She might have been chiseled from marble. Her delectable white skin glowed faintly in the starlight, and the shadows dancing across her body were intriguing. Slocum forced himself to look away from her and out across the desert leading to the mine, trying to catch sight of someone fleeing. He finally gave up the attempt and looked back at the naked woman.

"You'd better get some clothes on or you'll catch your death of cold."

"Death. That's what they want for me. I don't give up that easily. I'm not going to die and let Jerome get killed for nothing."

"Who wants you dead? Winthrop?"

The question took her by surprise. She looked at him, but he couldn't see her face. It was cast in shadow from the bright moonlight. For a moment, she said nothing, then she laughed harshly.

"Win would never do that. He doesn't have the balls."

"He never hesitated to hit you back in town," Slocum said.

"He's a coward. At heart, he's a yellow belly who jumps at his own shadows. He probably still wets his bed and—" Spring cut off her tirade and wrapped her arms around herself. If Slocum had put on a shirt or coat, he would have given it to her, but he was still bare to the waist himself. He felt the cold but ignored it.

"If not Winthrop, then who?"

"There are lots of people who don't think too highly of me in these parts. But you do, don't you, John? You like me a lot. A woman can tell that about a man."

Slocum wasn't sure Spring had a good idea why he had

accompanied her to the Silver Chalice. He had been on the
trail a long time and hadn't found a woman so lovely—and
so willing—in a month of Sundays. Bedding her had capped
off a day when he had become rich by robbing a road agent,
and she was hardly more than his well-deserved celebration.

"I ought to ride to town and find the sheriff."

"Why?"

He stared at her.

"Somebody gunned down Jerome, that's why. The town
marshal won't budge. Tombstone is the county seat, isn't it?
Or is it Bisbee?" He didn't cotton much to riding south to
Bisbee to let a sheriff know about a murder, but he would if
it came to that. He hadn't known Jerome and probably
wouldn't have liked him if he had, but the man was dead.
Somebody ought to pay for the murder.

"If you fetch the sheriff or the federal marshal, there'll
be no end of trouble. They're all in cahoots to do me out of
my mine, you know."

"No, I didn't." To Slocum's ear, this sounded a bit crazy.
He had no idea how much Spring was making up and how
much might be real, but one thing was for sure. Jerome was
dead.

"Are you going to stay here tonight, John? To defend me
if the killer comes back?"

"There might have been as many as three men. You piss
off that many folks in Tombstone?"

"More," Spring answered without hesitation. "You need
to . . . take me into your personal custody. All night long."
He saw her lips pull back in what might have been a feral
smile, or maybe the moonlight only made it appear that way.
Turning his back on her, Slocum walked in a large arc, studying the ground. Fifty yards away he saw fresh horse dung
where the killer had tethered his horse before attacking
Jerome. He dropped to hands and knees and looked closer.

"What did you find?"

"One rider. I saw what I thought were muzzle flashes from three guns, but it must have been one gunman fanning his six-gun as he ran."

"One man shooting at me," Spring mused.

"He was shooting at Jerome," Slocum said sharply. "I've got to get going or I'll never be able to track him. With this wind, the sand will blow over his trail."

"I can make it worth your while if you stay," she said seductively. She reached out with icy fingers to brush across his cheek. Slocum wondered if he touched her tit, would it would be this cold, too?

"I'll saddle up and find the man who wanted to kill you," he said, changing his tack.

"That would be a good idea," Spring said, chewing on her lower lip. "You do that, John, and I'll give you a fine reward. As long as you want." She stepped closer and pressed her cold hand into his crotch. "Long, all night long. I promise. And that's one promise I never renege on."

Slocum barely noticed her now. He hurried back to the cabin and grabbed the rest of his clothes. He had his shirt and vest on by the time Spring returned. She lit a coal oil lamp, placed it on the table, and turned, still naked, to face him.

"You won't just ride away, will you? You'll come back for me?"

Jerome was murdered. He might have gotten off a couple shots, but he had probably been awakened when the gunman missed with his first couple shots. Jerome had been dry-gulched as sure as anything. Whatever reaction he might have had wasn't good enough to save his life.

"I'll find who killed him and why," Slocum vowed.

"And then you'll come back to me," Spring said, moving to him and pressing close. Even through his clothes, her body felt like ice. She kissed him, and Slocum felt himself responding. Then she broke off and looked at him with a smug expression that hardened his heart.

"Then it's settled," she said. "You'll do this for me, then come back. Go on, kill him. Whoever killed Jerome ought to die. There's no need to get the law involved, since they're all as crooked as whoever the killer is."

"Who killed him?" Slocum hoped the simple question would shock an answer from her, but she got a wary look to her and shook her head. Her auburn hair floated about her bare shoulders and made her look innocent. Slocum knew Spring Atkins was anything but that.

"I don't know."

Slocum was a good poker player, but he couldn't tell if she was lying. He gave her another quick kiss to forestall any more discussion, then slipped out into the cold, windy night. His mare protested being saddled but had rested enough not to balk. He rode to the spot where the killer had tethered his horse and then he rode away from there.

Riding in a zigzag pattern allowed him to find hints of a trail. The rider had galloped off, kicking up a passel of dust and tearing through the sparse vegetation in places. Where he had ridden through a patch of prickly pear cactus, probably inadvertently, Slocum got a good fix on the direction to take.

He sighted in on stars for his bearings because the physical tracks disappeared quickly. Even if the rider had left hoofprints, the wind would have erased them within an hour. Slocum pulled his bandanna up over his nose, this time to keep dust caught on the wind from tearing at his lips and cheeks. To his surprise, his lips were slightly swollen from the lovemaking. Until this instant he hadn't realized Spring had kissed him so hard.

As he rode, he thought about the lovely woman and her assured accusation that Jerome's killer had been after her instead. Slocum wondered about that. Anyone coming to camp would have known Jerome worked her mine. While the killer might have decided to eliminate any trouble from Jerome before going after Spring, it would have been easier to simply sneak up on Spring's cabin and shoot her. If Jerome responded, he could be cut down. If he didn't, for whatever reason, the killer could simply ride off without fear of getting shotgunned for his trouble.

Spring might be sure the killer had come for her, but Slocum doubted it. More likely, Jerome had been the target— and Jerome had died as a result.

He reached a road and had to choose which direction to head. Riding back and forth along the road, hunting for tracks for several minutes, proved futile. He couldn't find anything to assure him he had found the trail. The ceaseless wind had blown throughout the night, erasing any chance of finding the killer's tracks. After fifteen minutes, Slocum finally drew rein and stared out at the horizon. Faint glimmering for a new dawn turned the sky pinkish, then ignited colors for a sunrise that would have been spectacular if he had been the least bit interested. The rising sun did nothing for Slocum other than give him a chance to see what the darkness had hidden.

He was about to give up when he spotted a signpost leaning precariously to one side. He trotted over and read the crude lettering. The Blue Balls Mine lay in the direction of the low hills. A rueful smile came as he thought of the miner who had named the mine. Then he saw a pile of fresh horse flop that was hardly cool yet. Flies swarmed over it and gave him the trail again. Whoever had killed Jerome at the Silver Chalice had ridden almost straight as an arrow for the Blue Balls Mine. It wouldn't be the first time one miner had feuded with another to the point that lead flew like deadly birds.

He wondered how he ought to approach the mine. Riding up seemed dangerous when he thought the owner might have gunned down a man in cold blood. There wasn't enough cover to sneak up for a quick scout between him and the distant hill where the mine opened its dark mouth. If he circled and came over the hill where the mine burrowed in, he would spend the entire day in the saddle. It wasn't Slocum's way to be impatient, but he had the gut feeling that he must find out what was at the bottom of this well fast.

He rode forward slowly, giving anyone at the mine plenty of time to see him coming. For all he knew, he had already been spotted, since the entrance wasn't too far away. The steep road ended in a broad circular area.

The Silver Chalice had tons of drossy rock dumped into veritable mountains. This mine hadn't seen the same activity, and if Slocum was any judge, the nature of the discarded rock here warned of either low-grade silver ore or none at all. The Blue Balls Mine might be a worthless hole in the ground, making the name even more ironic.

He sat astride his horse, waiting to be noticed. He didn't get the itchy feeling that anyone studied him—or sighted him in down a rifle barrel. A curious nothingness existed here, as if the mine was abandoned. The horse and buckboard to one side of a small shack put that to the lie. Knocking on the door might gain him something, but Slocum wanted to be certain he didn't spook anybody. He had already discovered how trigger-happy folks were in this part of the country.

Movement caught his eye. He swiveled in the saddle and caught sight of a young woman coming from the mine. She carried a rifle, but it wasn't aimed in his direction. If anything, it looked as if it wasn't even loaded, judging by the way she carelessly swung it around. It never came in his direction, so Slocum didn't react.

"Howdy, ma'am," he called. As she stepped out into the morning sun, he blinked hard. Slocum rubbed his eyes and then squinted, thinking his eyes were playing tricks on him. It wasn't possible that he had ridden in a circle because this obviously wasn't the Silver Chalice. The sign nailed over the mouth of the mine confirmed that he had, indeed, ridden all night to a different mine.

But the woman was a dead ringer for Spring Atkins. Her

hair was shorter and bleached in strands, showing she had spent more time in the sun. Her complexion was that of a woman who worked outside in the dry air that both burned and desiccated her skin. But the bright blue eyes, the figure, the way she carried herself were identical to Spring Atkins.

"What can I do for you?" Even her voice had the same musical lilt to it as Spring's.

"I'm a bit lost. I took a wrong turn somewhere and—"

She lifted the rifle and pointed it at him. The way it moved told him it wasn't loaded. She moved it too easily. But then, she might have only a single round in the chamber, and all it took was a single shot to end his life.

"Not too likely. There aren't any branches in the road between here and Tombstone. In this part of the desert, there aren't many turns at all. You're lying."

"I was looking for the Silver Chalice Mine," Slocum said, taking a gamble. He saw her tense and lift the rifle to her shoulder. Her hands shook, and it wasn't from nerves. Simple mention of the mine made her so furious it seemed that sparks flew from her bright blue eyes.

"You got ten seconds to turn around and ride away or I drill you. And if you don't ride fast enough off my claim, I won't think twice about putting a bullet in your back, you son of a bitch."

"You're Spring's sister, aren't you?" From the stark fury on the woman's face now, he knew he had hit the bull's-eye.

"You damn well know it. You tell her to go to hell and take that no-account snake in the grass with her."

"You mean Jerome?" Slocum ducked as a bullet narrowly missed him. He reached for his six-shooter, but the woman jacked another round into the chamber and froze his hand halfway to the holster.

"I mean Jerome," she said coldly. "Spring can have him." She spat. "I sure as hell don't want any man who'd leave me for her."

"Because the Blue Balls doesn't have any silver in it?"

"He named the mine. I told him he wasn't getting any until he delivered some silver. He left me for her because the Silver Chalice is such a rich strike. He left me because her claim's proved and this one isn't. Not yet. But it'll be richer than hers ever could be."

Tears ran down the woman's cheeks, leaving behind dusty trails.

"I don't know much about that. Jerome was your man?"

"My husband, the son of a bitch. Why I ever married him is a mystery, and it's also the biggest shame of my life."

"Didn't catch your name."

"Summer Lorritsen, though I'm thinking of going back to my maiden name," she said, fire still in her eyes. "Jerome had it good here, if he'd only have worked."

Slocum said nothing. From what Summer Lorritsen said and the way she said it, he didn't much blame her husband for leaving. The problem was that Jerome had run off with his sister-in-law, though Slocum wasn't sure that was so. Jerome hadn't been too concerned when Spring showed up at the Silver Chalice with another man in tow. He had been more concerned with digging the silver from the rock than with who slept with the mine owner.

"I'm looking for a friend who passed through a little while back," Slocum said.

"I chased off a scroungy-looking man an hour back. He went that direction, though heaven knows why. There's nothing but desert out there. No water." Summer Lorritsen glared at him. "And I'm not giving the likes of you a single drop. Vamoose. Get on out of here."

Slocum touched the brim of his hat and headed in the direction Summer had indicated. He watched carefully for sign that the rider had come this way and that Summer hadn't lied, sending him into the depths of the desert to get even with him for knowing her sister. From the fire in her words, he doubted she knew the rider had killed her husband. If she had, she would have pinned a medal on his chest.

The thought caused Slocum to slow and finally turn in the saddle. He studied the mine for any sign that Jerome's killer was holed up nearby. Summer went back into the mine, leaning her rifle against the wall before she vanished. Faint sounds of a pick hitting rock echoed from the mine. If she was hiding the killer, she was acting all wrong—or putting on a perfect act. Slocum doubted she had feigned her anger.

He still waited for another ten minutes to see what happened. Summer came out of the mine, struggling with a wheelbarrow laden with ore. She began going through the rocks one at a time, checking for any flash of silver chloride. She was so intent on her chore that she never looked up to see Slocum watching.

Sure that Jerome's killer had ridden on, Slocum began walking his mare deeper into the desert. He sat a little straighter when he saw a freshly broken mesquite limb. A rider had passed too close, caught his jeans on a thorn, and left behind not only a piece of his pants but also a marker for Slocum to follow. The sap still oozed from the broken twig, telling him the rider was only minutes ahead.

Slocum checked his six-gun and then made sure his Winchester had a full magazine. It wouldn't pay to get into a shoot-out without the odds being as much in his favor as possible. Then to his surprise he unexpectedly found himself riding up onto the road leading to Tombstone. Rather than leaving the territory, the killer had ridden to town to get himself a shot or two of whiskey in celebration.

"Come on, old girl," Slocum said, urging his mare to a trot. "We can overtake him before he gets to town. There's no way I can pick him out of that bunch of owlhoots if he mingles with them."

Slocum had hardly begun to trot along when a flash of

gunmetal caught his attention. He slowed and went for his pistol. In that same instant he knew he had made a big mistake.

"I got the drop on you, Slocum."

"How do you know my name?" He raised his hands and turned to face the man with a rifle trained on him.

"You're the one who robbed Slow Joe. We pieced it together. You was dumb enough to show up in town flashin' a silver coin like we stole. Ain't nobody else had one, so we asked around till we found a gent who recognized you from up in Denver."

"Slow Joe?"

"Don't play dumb. Give us the silver coins you stole from him, and we'll let you go."

Slocum listened hard as two men moved about nervously, and he knew the outlaws had him in a cross fire. The glint of metal he had initially responded to had been from the robber who spoke. With guns trained on him from both sides of the road, he wasn't likely to escape. Dodge the opposite way and the other man would drill him.

"Why'd you kill Jerome Lorritsen?"

"What are you—?"

Slocum had an opening created by his surprise question. It was up to him to take advantage of it. He bent double as he tried to gallop away.

The bullet knocked him out of the saddle. His arms flailed as he fell to the ground, unconscious.

5

His face began to ache. He moaned, stirred, and tried to roll onto his side but couldn't. The strength had fled his body, but the prickly feeling on his face, the tiny tickling sensations, the way his face outright hurt, brought Slocum back to a semblance of consciousness. The intense sun hammered down squarely on his face. He grimaced and felt skin tearing away. The pain was secondary to the distant question echoing in his skull as to what was happening.

He brought shaky hands up to his face and felt the caked blood there. Ants provided the tiny tickly feeling. He brushed them off. He tried to open his eyes but couldn't. The blood had dried and matted shut both eyelids. Wincing, he scraped off the blood the best he could. This time before he opened his eyes, he jerked hard and got onto his side so the brilliance of the sun wouldn't blind him.

Slowly the world came into focus. At the center of it all was pain. If Slocum had a bone in his body that didn't outright hurt, he didn't know where it could be. Mostly, his head hurt like hell. He touched his temple again and came away with fresh blood. Pieces fit together, and finally he real-

41

ized the outlaws had shot him from the saddle. The instant of pain, the blackness enveloping him—that was all he remembered. Hitting the ground wasn't even a distant memory. He knew nothing of what had happened after the bullet struck him in the side of the head.

Pushing himself to hands and knees helped. He let the vertigo pass over him before standing. Another bout hit like a sledgehammer, but he had wobbled worse when he was on a bender. A few steps took him away from where he had been shot. He looked back over his shoulder at the spot and was amazed at the amount of blood that had been sucked up by the thirsty desert sand.

His hand went for his six-shooter. A moment of fear passed when he touched the hot metal cylinder. He drew his six-gun and checked it. It hadn't been fired. Then he remembered he really hadn't been in a gunfight. He had been the duck in a duck shoot. Slowly turning in a full circle, he saw that he was a dozen yards from the road. Of the two road agents he saw nothing. His horse was gone, too, along with his saddle and gear.

He touched his vest and found his brother Robert's watch. This was his only legacy from his older brother and it still rested in its proper spot. He even found another of the silver slugs. The outlaws hadn't bothered to search him. They hadn't even wasted an extra round on him to be sure he was dead. Slocum laughed ruefully as the thought crossed his mind that he must have looked well past dead, bleeding the way he had. The outlaws must have thought it was impossible for anyone to live with a wound like his.

He touched the bloody crease on his temple and winced again. It was more painful than it was dangerous. But being stranded on foot in the desert was likely to do him in. Without a horse or water, he wouldn't last another couple hours. Not a sign of any shade made it all the worse. The low-growing plants afforded him no succor. He couldn't even find a prickly pear to cut open and suck on the bitter juice.

He made his way back to the road, wondering if lack of blood or the heat boiling his brains caused his step to be so hesitant. It didn't matter. He was a goner.

"Like hell," Slocum said, his voice cracked. He got his bearings, guessed he had been unconscious for several hours, and headed down the road toward Tombstone. If he was turned around and went in the wrong direction, he'd be dead within an hour. Even if he had chosen the right way, he wasn't likely to survive much longer than that.

Refusing to simply sit down and die, he forced himself to put one foot in front of the other, over and over, the heat sucking away his strength, his head throbbing, his eyes blurred from sweat and sunlight. When he realized he had stopped sweating, he knew his time was up. Slocum stopped and forced himself to stand upright. He wobbled a considerable amount and waited for the wobble to go in the direction of Tombstone so he could take another stumbling step. This worked again. Then he fell to his knees, too dizzy to stand.

"You all right, mister? It's mighty hot, and it doesn't look as if you've got any water."

"Water," he said through crackled lips. Slocum had to laugh. His hallucinations were even of Spring Atkins. The voice was hers and the light brown hair carrying hints of red were identical. "You got any, Spring?"

"What? I don't have any springwater, but I do have enough to keep you alive. You just sit there. Let me move my buggy around."

He heard Spring snapping the reins on her team and moving the buggy up closer. He leaned against the wheel, wondering at how the hallucination could be so real. The spokes cut into his back, and the sound of the nervous horse was as real as if the horse actually stood only a few feet from him.

"Here."

He felt water against his lips. He sucked hard and choked.

Then he spit when the dirt in his mouth turned to mud with another gulp of the precious water.

"Not so fast. You'll bloat like any ole horse."

Slocum thought that was funny and tried to say so. He forced his eyes open and saw Spring holding a canteen just inches from his mouth. He couldn't get it all straight in his head. She didn't seem to know him and yet he knew her. It was a crazy hallucination brought on by sunstroke.

"Fever. I'm running a fever."

"Yes, yes, sunstroke. I know. I have worked as a nurse in my day."

"You never mentioned that," Slocum said. "But then I hadn't told you my name until after we'd spent the night together." He greedily swallowed more water. This time he didn't quite choke and wanted more. Lots more. All of it!

"I beg your pardon!"

The precious water vanished from his lips. He reached for the canteen and only fell over. His fingers brushed the flannel wrapper soaked in water so evaporation would keep the water a mite cooler. A desert bag would have been even better. He said so as he lay on his side in the dirt.

"You're mumbling and out of your head. Can you get into the buggy? You're too heavy for me to lift."

"Thought nurses could handle dead weight."

"You'll be dead if you don't get into the buggy."

Slocum felt something click deep inside his head. Spring Atkins was right. He wouldn't make it unless he did something. Going along with the fever dream was the best way of doing something, even if it was all make-believe.

"You're right, Spring."

"Stop calling me that!"

Her sharp tone forced Slocum to focus a little more. He took the canteen and sipped at the water. He felt the water knot hard in his belly, but he needed to get more into his body. His hands shook and his forehead burned, but his eyes focused better now.

"You're not Spring Atkins, are you? But you're the spitting image of her."

"She's my sister, more's the pity."

"Sister? Her sister's Summer Lorritsen."

"My, you've been busy. No wonder you tried to kill yourself in the desert. After meeting those two black widow spiders, you must have had an attack of good sense."

"You don't like them?"

The woman snorted. She got her arm around him and together they got Slocum to fall heavily into the buggy. He gripped the iron handle beside the hard seat and pulled himself upright. The canopy above knocked off his hat as he came to his full height.

"My, you're a tall one," the woman observed.

He introduced himself. If he was going to meet all the sisters, he might as well not make the same mistake twice.

"I'm Autumn Dupree."

"A pleasure," Slocum said. "Thanks for saving me. My bacon was just about fried to a crisp." He doubted he could stand yet, but he didn't have to. The buggy was secure under him, and he clung to the canteen as if his life depended on it. And it did. He was still woozy from dehydration. Autumn realized he needed the water more than she did and made no move to pry it from his weak fingers.

"How did you come to meet Spring and Summer?"

"Seems I got caught in the middle of a shoot-out. Jerome Lorritsen was at Spring's mine—"

"That damned Silver Chalice," grumbled Autumn.

"He was working the mine for Spring and somebody gunned him down. I tracked the killer to Summer's mine."

Autumn giggled this time.

"Jerome named it. Summer threatened to never sleep with him again until he pulled out a thousand dollars' worth of silver." Autumn chuckled at this and snapped the reins just a little harder than necessary to keep the horse pulling the doubly laden buggy. "He was a fool to ever marry Summer and an even bigger one to work for Spring."

"Were they . . ." Slocum wasn't sure how to delicately phrase it, but he wanted to find out more about Jerome and Spring's relationship. It hardly seemed likely it was simply employer-employee, not with Jerome being her brother-in-law and estranged from her sister, but this family had more kinks in it than a ball of steel wool.

"Who knows? Who cares? I try to avoid the lot of them. Every time I get involved with one or the other, nothing but woe befalls me. They're like that."

"Yeah, they're like that," Slocum agreed.

"How'd you end up on foot in the desert? I didn't see a horse dead along the road, but then it looks like you've been thrown. Hit your head on a rock?" Autumn glanced sideways at him, wanting to stare but not summoning the courage to do so. Slocum knew he looked more dead than alive, and the bullet wound in his temple contributed a good deal to that ugliness.

"Something like that," he said.

"But not exactly like that," she pressed.

"No, not exactly," Slocum said, unwilling to involve the woman. "You said you were a nurse. You work in Tombstone?"

"I used to be a nurse. Now I do a variety of things."

Slocum heard doors slamming in front of him and doubted he would get more information. Each of the sisters had a quirk. He wasn't sure if he didn't appreciate Autumn's most of all. She kept her own counsel, in spite of trying to pry into his business. Still, she had stopped to help him and deserved to know how he had ended up a half-past-dead bloodied mess.

"Tombstone," she said, as if it were a swear word.

"You tell me anything about the marshal?"

"What's to tell? He's for sale to the highest bidder, like everything else in town. You can get a decent drink—not watered down—at the Crystal Palace, or so I'm told. If you're looking for a whore, there are some honest madams who can accommodate you. Dutch Annie is supposed to have some skill. Or some I'm told."

"I'd prefer to get a place to rest up and get some victuals," Slocum said, amused at Autumn's appraisal of what he needed. In other circumstances, she would have been right. Now all he wanted was to rest up.

And to find a pair of outlaws who had stolen his horse and left him for dead in the desert.

"Then you'd best seek out Nellie Cashman. Good food, decent rooms for let, but she doesn't tolerate any shenanigans."

"Won't get any from me. I'm still too shaky to do too much."

"Then I will let you out by her restaurant. It's only a block from the Crystal Palace and a couple from the Birdcage Saloon. There are many others, but those are the most honest when it comes to pouring a drink."

"You sound like a real town booster," Slocum said.

This elicited a sniff of disdain.

"Hardly that. I listen and I know things. That's all. Here we are, Mr. Slocum." She put her dainty foot against the boards and pushed hard to bring the horse to a halt. The sudden stop almost tossed him from the buggy. Legs still shaky under him, Slocum climbed down and handed back the almost empty canteen.

"Much obliged, ma'am. You saved my life."

"I'm sure," she said, but there was no sarcasm in the words. Her blue eyes, so much like her sisters', bored into him and then became more appraising. "If you require further service, I stay in a boardinghouse just on the other side of the courthouse. It's a few blocks farther along the street. Good day, sir." With that, she got her horse pulling and rattled down the street in the direction of a three-story building Slocum figured to be the courthouse.

It took a bit of convincing to get a room. Nellie Cashman didn't like his looks, but the silver slug went a ways
toward convincing her to let him stay and even to draw a
hot bath for him. After Slocum had soothed away some of
the aches and pains and cleaned the blood off his face, he
felt almost human. He washed his duds in the bathwater
and wrung them out. It took only a few minutes in the afternoon sun for the clothing to dry. He felt damned near
whole by the time he stepped out into the twilight.

He considered going back to the saloon he had chanced
upon when first riding into Tombstone, but the Crystal Palace was nearby and his legs weren't up to walking even the
few blocks down the street.

He had a few coins rubbing together in his pocket that
would be enough to purchase a shot or two of whiskey.
Since Autumn Dupree had said this saloon didn't water its
drinks, he figured that would be a good way to spend his
money.

The saloon was packed shoulder to shoulder at the bar,
but the tables scattered around were mostly empty. From
what he could tell, anyone sitting at a table was fair game
for any of a half dozen tinhorn gamblers who would swoop
down like red-tailed hawks and strike up a poker game. If
he had had a few more of the silver coins from the robbery,
he would have indulged. Instead, he shouldered his way to
the bar and got himself a shot of whiskey and a cool beer to
wash it down.

The buzz around him rose and fell, but Slocum listened
closely to what was said nearest him. He wanted a hint about
the two robbers. Whatever he could find would go a ways
toward giving him the chance to put bullets through their
pair of black hearts. Nothing was lower down than a man
who would steal another's horse, unless it was a road agent
who'd do that and strand the rider in the desert to die.

The noise level dropped a mite when he heard the swinging door slam hard against the wall. Slocum looked up to

the mirrored wall behind the bar and vented a sigh. He drained his beer before turning to face Winthrop. The man was dressed in white so spotless that Slocum wondered if had been washed wearing the clothing. Just putting on an outfit like that would leave dirty finger smudges.

"I thought you'd left town," Winthrop said, his cold eyes fixed on Slocum.

"Thought I'd stop by for another beer." Slocum nudged the empty beer mug with his elbow. He kept his gun hand resting on his belt buckle. All he had to do was twitch and move a couple inches to draw. From the way Winthrop had singled him out, Slocum decided this was going to be the blowout.

"I'm going to kill you."

"That's mighty ambitious of you," Slocum said. "You get your fill of beating up women and decide you ought to do something like a man?"

"You son of a bitch! You had no right to interfere. The argument was between me and Spring."

"Spring didn't think so," Slocum said, intentionally infuriating Winthrop.

"I'm going to give you the beating of your miserable life," Winthrop said, rushing across the floor toward Slocum.

Although he had bathed, gotten the blood off his face, and felt worlds better, Slocum's head still ached like a son of a bitch and his legs proved a tad wobbly yet. Such a close brush with death took a while to get over, and there hadn't been sufficient time.

Winthrop rushed him like a charging bull, but Slocum's draw was fast enough. Winthrop crashed into him, then dropped to his knees when Slocum laid the barrel of his Colt Navy alongside the man's head. An ugly red spot formed that would eventually turn into a liver-colored purple and yellow bruise. If Winthrop lived that long.

Dead men didn't bruise.

"Hey, you can't go doin' that. You gotta—" The barkeep

clamped his mouth shut when he saw the thunderstorm expression on Slocum's face. Slocum knew the bartender had signaled someone to fetch the marshal, but this would be over long before the law showed up.

Slocum put his boot in the middle of Winthrop's snow white shirt and pushed hard. Winthrop sprawled on his back with Slocum's dark footprint on his chest. Blood oozed from the cut on his temple where Slocum had buffaloed him.

"What do I have to do to get free of you?" Slocum asked. "You beat up women, you threaten me. I can't let any of that stand."

He stood over Winthrop with his six-shooter drawn but not aimed at him.

The flair of fear on the fallen man's face told Slocum all he needed to know—as if he had hadn't guessed it already. Winthrop was a coward. The fear of dying was etched in every line of his face.

"You can't just shoot me."

"Why not?" Slocum kicked him hard in the ribs. His legs were so weak from his earlier ordeal that he didn't get enough power in the kick to make it satisfying, but it got Winthrop's attention. "You're like a foxtail burr under my saddle blanket. You're not too dangerous but you surely do annoy the hell out of me."

"You . . . you!" In spite of being supine on the floor, Winthrop went for his six-gun.

Slocum lifted his pistol to end the annoyance.

6

"John, don't!"

The cry rang out, cutting through the din in the saloon. Slocum looked up fast and saw Autumn Dupree standing in the doorway, gesturing frantically to him. He took it all in and shifted his aim just a tad before he fired. The bullet from his Colt drove down Winthrop's right arm, leaving behind a bloody gash. The man screeched in pain and was unable to close his fingers around the butt of his pistol.

"I'll kill you," Winthrop snarled. He reached over with his left hand, clumsily trying to drag out his six-shooter to carry through with his threat. Slocum considered making this one the final shot, but Autumn called out again to him.

"The marshal! He and two deputies are coming. They're coming for you, John. You've got to run!"

She burst through the door of the saloon and hardly glanced in Winthrop's direction. Slocum pushed her aside when she got close enough, then he took a step and kicked as hard as he could. The toe of his boot crashed into Winthrop's side. Slocum felt bone breaking. He had busted at least one rib and maybe two. The man gasped, rolled onto his side, and passed out from the intense pain. His face had turned a bleached muslin white and his breathing rasped out of his lungs.

"The law, John, the law," urged Autumn. "I heard 'em talking. They're after you. You don't dare kill him."

"It'd put us both out of our misery," Slocum said, glancing at Winthrop before turning away and letting Autumn pull him toward the rear of the saloon. A door he hadn't noticed there led to a hallway that made a quick right-angle turn. He and Autumn stepped out into the cold night air just as the marshal and his deputies barreled through the main door of the Crystal Palace.

"Why'd you stop me?" Slocum asked.

"Come on," she said, tugging at his arm. "They're meaner than stepped-on snakes, those lawmen."

"You didn't want me killing Winthrop. Why not?"

She faced him. Her blue eyes burned like sapphire in the bright moonlight. He'd thought Spring was a beauty. Autumn was becoming his favorite season, but he wanted answers.

"Me, I don't know if the marshal wants you or not, but if you'd gunned down Win back there, the law would be after you."

"What's it matter to you?"

She started to say something, then got shy all of a sudden. She turned from him and looked at the ground. Her shoulders hunched over just a mite, and she tried to say something twice before words finally sneaked out of her lips.

"There's something about you."

"I reckon you did me a favor," Slocum said. "Having his blood on my hands wouldn't be a good thing." He let the words come out, more to see how she responded than because he believed them. Gunning down Winthrop wouldn't have caused him to lose one second of sleep. If anything, he would have slept more soundly knowing a son of a bitch like that wasn't going to murder him while he was all wrapped up in his bedroll.

"No, it wouldn't. And you have such fine, big hands." Autumn reached out. Her dainty hands gripped Slocum's. Her fingers lightly traced over his palms and then worked up to his wrists. Now she looked at him, bolder, more demanding. "You're more of a man than he ever could be."

Slocum figured it out then. Autumn and Winthrop must have been lovers. She didn't want him killed, but she had reasons other than being unwilling to go to a former lover's funeral. Slocum hoped that he knew that reason. Autumn Dupree was a fine-looking woman, but then so were both of her sisters.

"Come on," she said, glancing over her shoulder. The marshal and a deputy supported Winthrop between them as they dragged the man from the Crystal Palace. Winthrop struggled feebly. Slocum wondered at that because the crease he had put on the man's gun hand wasn't enough to cause blood loss. Then he saw why. The deputy swung around and landed a slungshot just behind Winthrop's ear. The man sagged again, supported only by the marshal.

"They'll keep him in jail overnight," Autumn said. "May he rot there."

Before Slocum could say anything, Autumn steered him down the street to the next block. More saloons blared piano music out into the night. Raucous laughter filled the air, and the smell of stale beer and spilled whiskey made Slocum's nose twitch. He hadn't had much of a chance to wet his whistle, but having Autumn on his arm took away some of the need.

Some of that need.

"Let's set ourselves down and talk some," she said, sinking down to a bench in front of the post office.

He sat beside her, close enough so his leg pressed warmly into hers. The woman's voice was hardly audible over the carousing going on in nearby saloons.

For a moment, neither said anything. Slocum finally broke the silence between them.

"Why'd you keep me from killing Winthrop?"

"He needs killing, I suppose," Autumn said slowly. She laced her fingers together, unwound them, and then balled her hands in her lap. She kept her eyes averted. "He's a real disappointment to his ma and pa."

Slocum snorted. That was one way of saying it.

"John," she said, turning to him. Her face was hidden in shadows, and he could barely see the fine lines of her face. That her beauty was hidden disturbed him less than being unable to get a hint as to her mood, but her tone carried an urgency that put him on guard.

She reached out and took his hand in hers before continuing.

"She doesn't deserve it."

"What are you talking about?"

"Spring. My sister Spring. She doesn't deserve the Silver Chalice Mine. She might as well have stolen it from me."

"If you have a claim to it, there are plenty of lawyers in Tombstone who'd be willing to file all the court papers."

"I hate lawyers. They are the lowest of the low. They . . . they have to look up to see a snake's belly! They can put on a top hat and walk upright between a duck's legs. They—"

"You don't like lawyers," Slocum interrupted. "There's not much I can do to evict your sister. Possession counts for more than about anything else, especially if you have a shotgun to back up the claim. From what I could tell, the Silver Chalice is a rich mine."

"It might be about the richest in these parts. Goose Flats has holes punched in it all over the place. The hills surrounding Tombstone have even more dug into them, but the Silver Chalice is the one bringing forth the ore. Oh, there are several here in town that are richer, but the Silver Chalice has the potential to outproduce even the Good Enough." Autumn took a deep breath. Slocum would have been blind not to see the rise and fall of her bodice. Even shadow could not hide the delightful motion. "She stole it from me. Me and Andre."

"Your husband?"

"Pa gave us the mine because we were the only ones in the family to work there with him. But when he died, we brought him into town to the cemetery. It was a nice service, but I wondered why Spring didn't attend. She and Pa were always on the outs, arguing and carrying on, but he was blood. When Andre and I returned to the mine, we found out why."

"Spring had moved in?"

"During her very own father's funeral!" Autumn's outrage boiled over, and she squeezed his hand so hard he thought bones might break.

"The marshal wouldn't do anything about a claim jumper, even if it was your own flesh and blood?"

"She has forged documents. She showed what she said was Pa's last will and testament to a judge, and he was too blind to see that Spring's handwriting and that of the will were identical. The forgery wasn't good, not at all!"

"Good enough to convince a judge."

"I think she slept with him. That'd influence his decision, wouldn't it?"

Slocum tried to decide if she was being cagey or was just naive. Autumn didn't seem like the shrinking violet type to him, and he doubted anything in town happened without her knowing every detail.

"Reckon it could," he said, considering how well that lure had worked with him. For all he knew, it had worked with Jerome Lorritsen, too, though the man had seemed more interested in getting back at his wife, Summer, by flashing silver nuggets under her nose. Just what had brought the man to his death still puzzled Slocum.

"Help me get back what's rightfully mine," Autumn said. "You're the man who can do it. She . . . she trusts you.

Spring wouldn't expect you to do anything to dislodge her from that mine."

"What do you want me to do?" Slocum asked, now wary.

"You sound as if you think I want you to kill her. Don't be silly. In spite of all she's done, she's still my sister. She's my blood. What I want you to do is find that forged will and burn it. Destroy it. Tear it into tiny pieces and scatter it to the four winds. Without it, she wouldn't have a leg to stand on in court."

"You have some document to support your claim?"

Autumn paused, then shook her head.

"It'd be your word against hers about what your pa intended."

"Then you'll have to lure her away from the mine so I can hurry in and claim it, the way she did. If I'm there, she wouldn't be able to chase me off."

"You and your husband?"

"Andre?" Autumn sat a little straighter. "He's no longer a factor. He returned to France."

"He left you?"

"He said some hateful things about me and Spring."

Slocum understood what Andre Dupree might have said about not wanting to be in the cross fire between the two sisters. If he knew about Summer—and he probably did since nothing seemed to be kept quiet among the sisters—that might have added speed to his departure. Slocum had never been to France, but it had to be a powerful lot more peaceful than Tombstone or the squabbling over the Silver Chalice Mine.

"Are you divorced?"

"He abandoned me. I blame Spring for that. She stole the mine, and Andre wasn't man enough to stand up to her. He wasn't half the man you are, John. Help me. Get the mine back for me. It's what my pa would have wanted."

"I'll see what I can do," he said cautiously. His instincts

told him to try to catch up with Andre Dupree, no matter when the Frenchman had left. Getting out of Tombstone and away from the sisters was only common sense, but he couldn't get the time he'd spent with Spring out of his mind. In her way, Autumn was even lovelier. And what about Summer? She was a grieving widow now.

Slocum swallowed hard as a thought crossed his mind. All three of the sisters had lost a husband, mainly through violence centered at the silver mine.

"You're a dear," Autumn said, moving closer to give him a big kiss. "I knew I could count on you."

Before Slocum could do anything more, Autumn got to her feet and walked away. A dozen paces down the street, she looked back over her shoulder and blew him another kiss. Slocum watched in bewilderment. He had expected Autumn to offer the same inducement her sister had in return for his help. Shrugging it off, he decided each of the sisters was different in her own way.

Autumn might be the loveliest of the trio, but he still remembered Spring and the pleasurable hours they'd spent together. He wasn't sure if he didn't like her ways of persuasion best of all when compared with Autumn and Summer.

But there might be something more with Autumn Dupree. Slocum heaved himself to his feet and stepped out to the street, looking back at the Crystal Palace. That had been a mighty fine watering hole, but the water there would be tainted now after the run-in with Winthrop. Slocum turned toward another, smaller saloon and pushed through the doors to take a look around. The waitresses serving drinks here reminded him of the pretty waiter girls in New Orleans, only those fine fillies wore a lot less. Here in Tombstone there was more tease and less skin showing.

That suited him. It would divert the attention of anyone he got to talking. From the look of the crowd, only a drink or two would put most of them out flat on the floor. They had started drinking early and hadn't stopped.

"What'll it be?" The woman behind the bar was hefty and looked as if she could be the bouncer as well as the owner. The air of command about her cowed some of the men on either side of Slocum.

"Rye."

"Comin' up." She expertly slid a shot glass a foot down the bar so it stopped directly in front of Slocum, then poured without spilling a drop.

"You're mighty good at pouring," he said.

"That's not all I'm good at."

Slocum smiled. He didn't doubt it.

He considered the men around him as potential sources of information, then decided whatever he got from them would be filtered through a half bottle of whiskey and as unreliable as a water well in the middle of the desert.

"Go on, ask," the barkeep said. "What's eating you? Ole Maude, here, that's me of course, knows the itch and how to scratch it."

Slocum considered for a moment, then sipped at his whiskey. It wasn't too bad. He decided the information he'd get from Maude would be about the same—and not watered down.

"I find myself in the middle of a family squabble," he began. He clamped his mouth shut when Maude laughed, deep and rich and long. Then she laughed even harder, until tears rolled down her cheeks, forcing her to use the bar rag to mop them up.

"The sisters. You blow into town and get caught up in their whirlwind."

"You know?"

"You're not the first. I heard tell of a gent described 'bout like you who'd taken up with Spring Atkins. I hope your dick doesn't fall off. No tellin' what that girl's contracted, sleepin' round the way she does. Even among whores, I've never seen a woman so quick to strip and slip into bed." Maude controlled her mirth and then said, "Your dick gettin' all poxy is maybe the least of your worries. That one'll take your balls and keep 'em in a lockbox, she will."

"I got that impression. After Jerome got himself killed, I tried to track down his killer."

"Do tell? I hadn't heard that." Maude served more whiskey and came back to Slocum. "I'm willin' to trade information. That's my actual stock and trade here, not sellin' whiskey to these reprobates." She waved a muscular arm around to encompass the entire saloon and its patrons. "You know who killed him? Jerome wasn't much brighter than a yoked up mule, but I liked him."

"Tracked the killer to Summer's claim and lost the trail there."

"Yup, you got yourself all mixed up in a real dust devil. Spring and Summer." Maude eyed him closely. "But it's not 'bout them you're all hot and curious, is it? Want some more? A half bottle? That's ten dollars."

Slocum dropped the money on the bar but only got another shot. He figured the rest of the money went for information.

"Autumn Dupree is Tombstone's number-one snoop. Nothing goes on here without her knowin'," Maude said.

"Sort of like you?"

Maude pulled herself up to her full five-foot-two height and thrust out her ample chest, looking all riled.

"No, sir, not like me. I provide a needed service and give full measure in every exchange."

Slocum said nothing. He had paid ten dollars for a second shot of rye. If Maude was telling the truth, more would be forthcoming.

"She lost her husband to her sister."

"Spring?"

"Must have been. There was some unpleasantness about their papa's funeral. Spring decided to squat on the claim. Not sure what Andre did, but he mighta throwed in with the wrong sister."

"You mean Autumn killed him? She said he'd gone back to France."

Maude laughed. "Never heard it said like that before. I think he's in an unmarked grave out on Goose Flats, but he mighta gone back to the Continent. If he went, I wish he'd a took me. I never have seen Paris."

"It's lovely in the spring," Slocum said. "Or so I've heard."

Maude looked at him for an instant, then burst out laughing again. It didn't take much to get her tears flowing.

"You're a card, mister. I like that in a man. Truth is, I like most things in a man."

"You're saying Spring could have killed him?"

"Wouldn't put it past her. She's got a mean streak a mile wide that goes all the way down to her black heart."

Slocum nursed his whiskey a bit more, thinking about what Maude had told him. A few details differed, but the story ran along the same trail as the one Autumn had told him. Spring had stolen the Silver Chalice Mine while her sister and brother-in-law were at the funeral and somehow Autumn's husband had disappeared afterward. If Autumn had killed him for leaving her and taking up with Spring, Slocum knew he'd have to watch his back. Autumn would as likely turn on him if the need arose. But from all he had learned, it seemed more likely Spring had killed Andre Dupree.

Or Andre had just gone back to France. If Slocum had a lick of sense, he'd leave town, too, if not for France then for somewhere far enough away that Spring, Summer, and Autumn weren't a concern.

He finished his whiskey and set it down on the bar with a loud click.

"Much obliged."

"Come on back anytime you got more to pass along—or you need to know more. Ole Maude's a gold mine of gossip 'bout purty near everyone in Tombstone."

"I'll do that," Slocum said.

As he got to the door, Maude yelled above the din, "Come on back even if you don't wanna gossip. We kin do a lot more together!"

Her boisterous laughter followed him into the cold desert night.

7

"Oh, you're the finest, John. I knew you'd help me." Autumn Dupree threw her arms around Slocum's neck and almost strangled him as she hugged him tightly. She pressed close and moved sinuously, like a cat rubbing up against a post. As quickly as she had grabbed him, she released her hold and stepped away, looking flustered. Autumn looked around guiltily. "I was overwhelmed," she said. "I didn't mean to make a public scene."

"Nobody noticed," Slocum said, knowing that a dozen people had. The sight of Autumn walking down the street drew attention. Her hugging a man in plain view was something that would keep the gossip buzzing for days. When it reached Maude's ears, its life might be extended for weeks.

"Oh, good," she said, trying to sound prim. Her words might have reached that level, but her appearance didn't. Her hair was mussed and her lace collar was askew. She self-consciously adjusted everything and looked flustered. A quick movement over her skirt smoothed out any wrinkles that might have mysteriously appeared due to her exuberant indiscretion.

"Destroying the will isn't going to be enough," Slocum said. "I can probably do that much, but you need legal documents to support your case in court."

"Court," Autumn said derisively. "Spring has at least one judge wrapped around her little finger. She might have more. They are such venal men."

"Find the judge who's jealous of another. They're politicians. Play one off against the other."

"My, I never thought of it that way," Autumn said. "I'm so glad you agreed to help me." She looked up at him, her bright blue eyes gleaming. A quick circuit of her lips with only the tip of her tongue told Slocum she was playing with him like a cat with a mouse. He didn't much care, but she hadn't started to purr yet.

"It might take a while," he said. "Spring isn't the kind to leave such important papers laying about."

"Her bed," Autumn said. "Look under her bed. In the mattress. Somewhere around it. That's where she could keep a close watch on anything important."

Slocum tried not to laugh at that. Autumn didn't realize what she was suggesting about her sister. Or maybe she did. In some ways, Slocum felt out of his depth dealing with the sisters.

"I'll let you know when I find the will."

"Burn it. Don't try to bring it back. That would only confuse matters more if you tried to prove to a judge—any judge—that it was a forgery. Spring mustn't be allowed to use it again."

Autumn tipped her chin upward and her eyes half closed as if she expected him to kiss her. People on both sides of Toughnut Street watched them with obvious curiosity. Even the landlady of the boardinghouse where Autumn lived was peering through barely parted curtains. A sigh of resignation escaped Autumn's lips when Slocum stepped back and pulled the reins free of a hitching post. He walked his horse away from the woman, aware of dozens of eyes following his departure. In this part of Tombstone not much went unnoticed. Slocum ignored the stares and found the trail leading to the Silver Chalice Mine.

The entire way he turned over in his head what he would say to Spring when he reached the mine. Coming right out and telling her that Autumn had sent him to steal back the richest silver mine in the area hardly seemed the proper approach, since folks in Tombstone weren't sure exactly what happened to Andre Dupree. Slocum wouldn't put it past Spring to have gunned him down, especially if he had disappointed her in bed—or tried to double-cross her.

He drew rein a hundred feet from Spring's cabin and waited for her to notice he was there. Surprising a miner was never a good thing to do, because they mostly had itchy trigger fingers and were a suspicious bunch. He couldn't discount Spring Atkins sharing those traits.

Slocum sat a little straighter when the door opened and a rifle barrel poked out. He lifted his hands away from his sides to show he wasn't going for his pistol.

"Spring? It's me, Slocum."

The door opened wider, and he saw her oval face peering out down the rifle barrel. She kicked the door all the way open and stepped out, but never let the rifle waver from its target.

"You're back?"

"Couldn't find Jerome's killer," he said. "I tracked him across half the desert and lost him."

"You're back!" She lowered the rifle and let out a whoop of glee. He hadn't expected the reaction.

Slocum urged his horse forward and dismounted, only to find himself with an armful of warm, willing woman. She lavished kisses all over his face until he was gasping for air. Hands around her trim waist, he lifted her off her feet and set her down at arm's length.

"I'm glad to see you, too," he said. "I wasn't expecting a welcome like that."

"I worried so," she said. "I thought you might have been killed, too. Whoever killed Jerome was a mean cayuse."

That wasn't the description Slocum would have used. Spring waved the rifle around so he had to reach out and take it from her. She didn't put up a fuss at all, which let him relax a mite more. Whatever weapons she had now were only those God had given her. Slocum was sure he could deal with those.

"I wanted to be sure you were all right," he lied.

"I knew you'd come back!" She hugged him again but this time quickly released him and took the rifle from his hands. "Come on inside out of the sun. It'll be the death of you standing in the noonday heat like this." She linked her arm with his and guided him toward the cabin.

Slocum had to admit it was cooler inside.

"All I've got is some water, but it'll go a ways toward easing your thirst. I wish I had some whiskey to offer."

"This is fine," Slocum said, sipping at the water Spring had sloshed into a tin cup. The wet against his chapped lips gave him new strength. As the woman chattered on, he took a good look around the single room, hunting for possible hiding places. A sheet or two of paper could be stuffed about anywhere. In several places Slocum noticed that Spring had crammed newspaper into cracks in the walls to seal them. A fake will might be a good way of plugging such a leak, too.

And then there was the rock-hard mattress Autumn had mentioned. The lumpy mattress could hold just about anything, he reckoned. He snapped his eyes away from the bed to keep from giving Spring the wrong idea. As pleasant as it might be rolling around on the mattress with her, it was the middle of the hot afternoon—and it was mighty hot. Even stripped down to bare skin, Slocum wasn't up for such sweaty activity unless it was necessary to retrieve the bogus will.

"I need you, John," she said in a low, husky voice. She stared intently at him, but it wasn't with lust. "With Jerome dead, I need someone to look after my best interests."

"And work your mine?" The instant he said this, he saw her face light up and knew he had hit the bull's-eye.

"That would be wonderful, if you could do that. You have mining experience, don't you? Yes, I can tell. You've got the look of a man who can swing a pick and follow a vein of ore until it peters out."

"I've done my share of mine work," Slocum admitted.

"Blasting, too?"

He nodded. It wouldn't have mattered to the woman if he had grown two heads and turned greener than a mesquite leaf. Her imagination ran away with her, having him in the mine dragging out tons of ore a day that would make her rich. He had done enough mining in his day to know it was backbreaking work and not a job he was physically suited for. He stood a little over six feet tall and had to wear a hat or cut the top of his scalp off in the low-roofed mine. There was never a reason to bore out the roof unless an ore vein ran there. Every pound of rock had to be moved. He knew many of the tricks to keep from hauling the drossy rock out. Using the rocks pried loose from the walls as support for the mine roof was one of those techniques that saved time and sore muscles. Finding wood for supports in this part of the country was hard. Pine trees from mountains fifty miles off were barely adequate—no soft wood like pine made for good supports, and hardwood was a commodity too expensive for even the best of mines.

"If you get to work right now, you'll find it a cooler way to while away the hottest part of the day."

"Never thought on mining as a way of whiling away the hours," he said.

"Oh, you'll work—but there are compensations that go beyond money." Spring turned and made a point of unfastening the top button on her blouse. Seeing that she had his complete attention, she unfastened another and another to show the warm white swell of her breasts. "My, it is hot, isn't it?"

"Getting hotter by the minute."

"And harder," she said. Before he could reply, she added, "You don't want it to get too hard or you'll never swing that pickax in the mine. Go on over to the Silver Chalice and get to work. When you're done for the day, I'll have some grub waiting for you." She grinned lewdly. "There'll be a special dessert, too. Very special."

Slocum knew that his chance to search the cabin would come if he bided his time. Working for Spring Atkins and dragging silver ore from her mine was the only way he could get the chance.

"What's the job pay?" he asked as he stood at the door, ready to go to work.

"You won't have any complaints," Spring assured him. She shimmied a little, her shoulders slipping back and forth until her blouse slipped down to reveal even more of the deep valley that so tantalized him. "Now, you get on to work. Don't slack off. Jerome didn't, and I expect no less from you."

She closed the door behind him as he stepped into the intense heat of the Arizona sun. Slocum pulled his hat down to shield his eyes, made certain his horse had shade and water, and then walked to the mine. He hunted for any trace that someone else had been in the mine recently other than Spring, and found nothing. From the scuff marks, he wasn't certain she had even bothered to enter the mine after Jerome was gunned down.

At the mouth, he looked around, squinting against the sun as he sought out hidden gunmen. Jerome Lorritsen's killer had been bold as brass, walking up and shooting the miner the way he had. Slocum doubted the killer would repeat his crime in that fashion. Better to lie in wait, get a decent shot with a rifle, and dispatch yet another obstruction in the way of claiming the Silver Chalice. That was the only reason he could see that Jerome had died—he worked the mine for Spring. From the way Summer acted, she didn't have another beau to replace her dead husband. When Slocum had met her, she hadn't seemed to be aware her husband had died. If she had killed him or had a boyfriend do it for her, she would have faced Slocum down, daring him to prove she had anything to do with the crime. There would have been no way she could have contained herself declaring her innocence.

The wicked flee when no man pursueth.

The three sisters were each different, but that didn't mean Slocum couldn't figure out what went on inside their lovely heads. He doubted Summer knew of Jerome's murder.

He hung up his six-shooter on a nail just inside the entrance to the mine. A miner's hat with a metal crown would keep him from banging his head too much as well as provide a spot for him to put the miner's candle. He took several from a ledge and worked to get the wick of one lit. The flickering yellow light wasn't as good as a lantern, but there wasn't as much smoke, either. If necessary, he could light a second candle to aid his work. In one mine where he had worked for close to a month, miners were allowed only one candle per ten-hour shift. From that experience he knew the candles were good for only a couple hours.

The lack of light had hindered all the miners on that job, so they had taken to pooling their candles so there would be continual light for the entire shift by lighting only one at a time. This hardship had bonded them together into a gang that watched one another's backs. Although it had never been said, Slocum knew those other four men on his shift would have died for one another. That friendship had worked against the mine owner. When he tried to add hours to the shift and cut their pay, the crew worked together to prevent that.

Slocum didn't know if wanted posters were still out for the five of them in Virginia City, but he didn't want to find out by returning there anytime soon, either.

Walking slowly into the mine, he ran his fingers along

the broad streak where the horn silver—silver chloride—
had been reamed out. Whoever had begun work hadn't
been too skilled and had left behind huge smears of the ore.
The deeper into the mine Slocum explored, the more expert
the mining became. He found layers where the vein had
been dug clean out, leaving behind only occasional flashes
of the ore. None of this would be worth scraping away,
unlike that near the mouth of the mine.

Tiny rooms opened into long narrow shafts. He found two
larger chambers of a size where a dozen miners could work
at a time. The honeycomb of rooms and tunnels had been
built over long months of work, and yet flashes of silver
still showed in the walls.

By the time he reached the far end of the underground
maze that was the Silver Chalice, he knew that Spring Atkins was one rich woman. Not only had a great deal of silver been removed from this mine, even more remained
locked in the hard rock. There might be hundreds of thou-
sands of dollars still in the ground, waiting to be teased out
with pick and blast.

He sat on a rock and looked around at the sparkling ore
running like arteries through the mountainside and wondered if Autumn and Spring might come to an agreement
about splitting the money so much silver could bring. There
was more than enough metallic wealth here for two women.
Slocum guessed Summer could be included and all three
would live comfortably till the end of their days.

Then he knew it didn't work that way. When it came to
money, there was never enough. The richest men wanted
more, not because they could spend it or needed it but simply because they didn't have it. He saw no reason to believe
the women would react differently to the lure of such im-
mense wealth. Slocum heaved to his feet and splashed some
hot candle wax around. He gingerly removed the miner's
helmet and saw that the candle had burned down to a nubbin. Using the sputtering flame, he lit another candle, placed

it in the pool of hot wax left from the first candle, and then settled it on his head. When he got down to work—if he did—the candle would be better placed on a ledge near where he extracted the ore. For now, this crude arrangement suited him better, even if rapid movement caused the flame to gutter.

The dust in the mine was making him cough, and hot as it was outside, the sight of the blue sky and the open spaces was what he needed now more than being enclosed in a rocky coffin.

Even if that coffin was almost pure silver.

He explored a few more drifts off the main tunnel and saw they had not gone far before petering out. The primary ore vein had started at the surface and ran directly into the mountain, with a couple major diversions where the large rooms had been chewed out of the mountainside. That made working the mine all the easier. No long days needed to be spent following a possible vein, only to find that it went nowhere.

As he got closer to the mouth of the mine and the brilliant sunlight that made him squint, Slocum slowed and then stopped altogether. Something wasn't right, and he couldn't put his finger on it.

He snuffed out the candle and placed the miner's hat and the spare candles back where he had gotten them. Stride long, he bent low to keep from banging his head against the rocky roof. As he reached out to retrieve his six-shooter he knew what was wrong.

The pistol was gone.

The whine of a bullet ripping through the air was the last thing Slocum heard as he jerked backward and fell to the ground.

8

Slocum moaned and stirred, trying to sit up. More slugs ripped through the air above him and forced him flat again. His head felt as if it would explode, but a cautious investigation showed he had done nothing more than bang it against the ground. The bullets whining just inches away from him, though, promised more permanent damage.

He slithered deeper into the mine and sat up, back against the cold rock wall, to wait for the dizziness to pass. He'd have quite a knot on the back of his head, but this was the least of his problems. He had no way out of the mine except through the opening still in the sights of someone's rifle. Slocum inched up the wall and grabbed the miner's helmet. Holding it front of him, he worked his way toward the mouth of the mine.

The bullet hit the helmet smack-dab in the center and ripped it from his hand to clatter away into the mine. If he'd been wearing the helmet, he would have had a hole through his brain. Slocum hunkered down and tried to get a look outside. If he faced only one sniper, he had a chance. Some kind of diversion might be enough to let him make a run for

it. If he fired enough rounds, the sniper would have to reload. If there were several gunmen outside, Slocum wouldn't
make it ten feet before they plugged him.

He chanced a quick look out but saw nothing. He flinched
as he tried a second look. Exploding stone fragments in
front of his face ripped at his flesh and left a bloody scratch
on his cheek. Standing quickly, he chanced another quick
look outside. The blazing sun dazzled him, but he caught
the glint of sunlight off the metal rifle barrel poking around
the edge of Spring's cabin. He couldn't tell whose finger
was on the trigger.

Several more quick shots drove him back. If that was the
only rifle trained on him . . .

There was no way to tell. Slocum faded back into the
mine to look for a weapon. He found several picks. Hefting
a rock hammer made him feel a little better, but this was an
infighting weapon and wouldn't serve him well against a
Winchester. He tucked it into the waistband of his jeans and
hunted further. In a crevice he found several sticks of dynamite and some waxy black miner's fuse, but no blasting
caps. Storing the dynamite inside the mine was asking for
trouble, but whoever had put the explosive there had had
the good sense not to store the blasting caps there, too. Heat
didn't affect the dynamite—it only exploded from a sharp
concussion. The best way of setting off the dynamite if he
didn't have a blasting cap was to put a bullet or two into
the sticks.

He didn't have his six-gun, either.

Slocum replaced the dynamite, thinking of ways to use
it to his advantage. It would be suicidal, but he might swing
a pick onto a half stick and create such a commotion, kicking up a dust cloud and sending out stone fragments, that he
could escape. The only problem he saw with this plan was
trying not to detonate all of the dynamite. If he swung a
pick to set off the explosive, he was likely to blow himself
to Kingdom Come.

Nothing else in the mine suggested itself to him as a weapon. Slocum hurried back to the mouth of the Silver Chalice, since he didn't want his attacker to come into the mine, guns blazing. There was nowhere to hide and certainly nowhere to run if he got trapped at the far end of the mine. His only hope lay in waiting for a chance to run away from the mine and taking it.

For an hour he sat, wondering why the sniper didn't simply walk up with rifle blazing and finish him off. The sniper had stolen his six-shooter and had to know he wasn't armed. Slocum fingered the miner's pick, then drew it out and idly used the sharp point against the rock wall. Tiny cascades of dust floated on the air and tiny bits of stone fell to the floor. If he had to, he could pick out fist-sized rocks and throw them at the gunman shooting at him. He might die, but it beat starving to death in the mine.

The more he thought about it, the less sure he was of his attacker. Spring Atkins might have turned on him. Somebody might have ridden from town and told her he was only hunting for the will so he could destroy it. Slocum thought only Autumn and he knew of the real reason he had returned to the Silver Chalice, but someone might have overheard them scheming. If Maude, only a barkeep, knew everything that happened in Tombstone, gossip had to be a great entertainment for the miners.

Spring might be shooting at him, or someone else might have already killed her and be working hard to kill him. There were few honest men in Arizona Territory and even fewer in Tombstone. The Silver Chalice was a prize to be won and cherished.

Whoever had gunned down Jerome might have taken it into his head to remove everyone else at the mine. If a killer moved in and laid claim to the Silver Chalice, who would dispute it? A squatter with a rifle and the nerve to use it might hold a winning hand. Autumn had lost her claim in court, and Summer's involvement was a mystery to Slocum. Another forged quitclaim or even a big bribe to the land office clerk in Tombstone might be all it would take for someone else to shoot his way into legal ownership.

When the sun began to sink low on the horizon, Slocum knew he had to get away. Whoever had shot at him would realize how easily he might escape in the dark and come for him before the moon rose. He gripped the miner's pick, took a deep breath, and ran from the mine.

He got only a few paces before the furious gunfire drove him back into the mine.

Panting, he leaned against the cold stone wall. When he regained his breath, he'd have to try again in spite of it being suicidal. Slocum had gotten his feet under him and was preparing for another attempt when gunfire of a different tenor sounded. He knew the report well. Someone was firing his Colt Navy. And then he was bowled over and landed flat on his back again, this time with a struggling body atop him.

He tried to swing the pick, but his arm was pinned to the ground. Reaching up, he grabbed and felt his fingers sliding through long hair. He recoiled and then got a better look at the person pinning him down.

"Autumn!"

"Here, take this horrid thing!" Autumn Dupree struggled to get off him and thrust his six-shooter toward him. He didn't have to be asked twice to take it.

He knocked out the cylinder and saw five rounds had been fired.

"I shot my way in," Autumn explained. "I didn't hit anything. I don't think I did."

"Too bad." To his surprise Autumn had his gunbelt slung over her left arm. She handed that to him as if it would turn into a snake and sink inch-long fangs into her tender flesh. He worked to get cartridges from the belt. Not for the first time he was glad he had rechambered the Colt Navy to take cartridges rather than having to load each round separately with bullet and black powder.

He slung the belt around his middle and fastened it securely after he had reloaded.

"How many are out there?"

"I . . . I don't know," she said. "I only now rode from town to see how you were doing. It was foolish, I know, but I want this mine! As I got closer, I heard gunfire. Lots of it."

"How'd you get my six-shooter?"

"I found it over by your horse. I wondered why you'd just toss it onto the ground, then I heard more gunfire and knew you were in danger."

Slocum's mind raced. Autumn didn't know how many gunmen were firing into the mine, but she had changed the odds considerably. It was twilight outside now, and his attackers had lost the chance to rush him. With the gun in his rock-steady grip, they'd pay with their own lives if they made a frontal assault. Their chance to kill him had come and gone. If they had rushed him earlier, he would have been defenseless.

"Was it your sister doing all the shooting? Or were there others?"

"I just don't know, John. Really I don't. I had to help you and I brought you your gun and I hate it and we're going to die, aren't we?"

"Not now," he said, trying to calm her. She shook with emotion but held back her tears. "You stay close behind. I need to draw their fire to find where they're shooting from. I can force them to duck, and that'll be our only chance to get away."

"The horses are still on the far side of the cabin."

Slocum had seen a gunman firing around the side of the cabin. He asked Autumn if she had seen him.

She shook her head. "I didn't see anyone. When I got closer to the mine, bullets came from behind me. From that direction." She pointed toward the mound of discarded rock separated from the silver chloride ore.

Slocum nodded, getting a clearer picture in his mind. Anyone behind the small mountain of dross could command both the mouth of the mine and the cabin. If anyone came up the road to the mine, the gunman could swing around and take a potshot at them, too. But the strength of the position was also its weakness. If Slocum could move about freely outside the mine, he could pin down the gunman since there wasn't any other cover nearby. It was the pile of drossy rock or nothing.

"Let's go," Slocum said. "You make a beeline for the cabin, get behind it, and have our horses waiting."

"Be careful, John. Please."

The time had passed for such concerns. Slocum took a deep breath, then dashed out, six-gun leveled. He squeezed off a shot at the first hint of a rifle coming around the pile of depleted ore. Then he began fanning his six-shooter, sending tiny tornadoes into the air in front of the hidden gunman. Try as he might, Slocum couldn't tell who'd been firing at him. Then his pistol came up empty, and he put his head down and ran for all he was worth.

It took the bushwhacker a few seconds to realize Slocum was no longer returning fire. By the time the rifle opened up again, Slocum was safely around the side of Spring's cabin, where Autumn waited with their horses.

He nodded once in appreciation. She hadn't driven out in a buggy but had a decent saddle horse under her. Slocum vaulted into his own saddle, silently pointed for Autumn to ride on, and then drew his Winchester from the saddle sheath. He levered in a round, went to the corner of the cabin, and took a shot in the direction of the debris. The difference in report was enough to keep the sniper back and under cover.

Slocum considered an all-out attack and then wheeled about to gallop after Autumn. The cabin blocked a direct shot. By the time the sniper had screwed up the courage and come after them, Slocum and Autumn would be out of range. A descent into an arroyo further protected them, even as the sandy bottom made it more difficult for their horses to maintain a fast gait.

"Slow up or the horses will break a leg," he called to the woman. She drew back on the reins and brought her gelding to a walk. The horse's flanks were lathered and its nostrils flared as mighty lungs sucked in air.

"Are we safe?"

"Not likely," Slocum said. "We keep riding, but keep the pace down in case we need to run for it on level ground." The arroyo wended around and soon spilled out into more level, sandy desert.

"We ought to go back to town," Autumn said. "We should fetch the marshal and have whoever was shooting at us put in jail immediately."

"Did you see your sister anywhere?"

"Spring? No, I didn't. I thought she must have hired whoever it was shooting at us and didn't want any part of the killing. She'd think that would keep her conscience clear." Autumn snorted like the horse she rode. "For all I know, she doesn't even have a conscience."

"You're sure it wasn't Spring firing at us?"

Autumn shook her head.

Slocum rode in silence for a spell, thinking hard. While he had been in the mine examining the veins of silver chloride, a small army could have ridden up. Anyone could have taken Spring hostage—or the sniper could have been someone Spring had cozied up to. But why would she want him dead after he had agreed to help mine the silver? It didn't make sense.

"Who killed Jerome Lorritsen?" he wondered aloud. Autumn twisted in the saddle and looked at him.

"Does it matter?"

"It does to Jerome," Slocum answered. Surprisingly, it mattered to him, also. He had seen more than his share of death, both in the war and after. Some of the corpses had come at his hand. He remembered how close Winthrop had come to being yet another in a long chain of death trailing all the way back to Calhoun County, Georgia, and the Slocum family farm. One more death ought not matter.

Somehow, Slocum felt he was responsible for Jerome's death, and he wouldn't stop until he found the reason—and the man's killer.

The road back to Tombstone appeared as if by magic, and the two of them rode into town, reaching it just before dawn.

"Let's go to my room," Autumn said. "We have a lot to talk over."

"Your room? That'll ruin your reputation if the landlady sees us."

"We're past such concerns," Autumn said. "Someone is trying to kill us!"

"How'd you come to be in a position to rescue me?" Slocum asked. He watched the woman's face closely but got no hint as to the truth.

"There. We can go in the back way. My room is just off the kitchen."

Autumn dropped to the ground and tied her horse to an iron ring mounted on the support post for the back porch. Slocum tethered his horse, too, and followed her inside. Already the half dozen other boarders were stirring. It wouldn't be long until the landlady began fixing breakfast.

"This isn't a good idea," Slocum said.

Autumn grabbed his wrist and pulled him along behind her, then turned, pushed him into the room, and firmly closed the door, as if this action would put his concerns about her reputation to rest.

"Don't be silly. Nothing's going to happen." She hesitated, her eyes going a little bit wider. "Is it?"

"Who did you tell I was going out to the Silver Chalice?"

"No one!"

Her adamant denial rang true. He saw no gain for her if someone put a bullet or two in him. After all, who else would be damn fool enough to go hunting for a will so he could destroy it? Autumn needed him.

"Why'd you come after me?"

"I was worried, John. The more I thought about Spring and her ways, the more I knew I could be of help it there were trouble."

She stared at him with those guileless blue eyes and made him believe.

"Thanks for pulling my fat from the fire. There wasn't any way I could ever get out of that mine. Whoever had me penned up had taken my gun. That was quick thinking on your part bringing it to me."

"Thank you," she said, smiling almost shyly. "I didn't know how to use it, but you certainly did."

If Autumn had taken the gun, he saw no reason for her to come back to save him. Let the killer have his way. Slocum knew how close a shave he'd had getting trapped in the mine.

"You never saw your sister?"

"Nowhere. I think she's in cahoots with whoever tried to shoot you. What else makes sense?"

Slocum rolled that around in his head but couldn't come to a conclusion. Spring had no reason to kill him. But then she'd had no reason to kill Jerome. Someone else was out to drive her from the mine and take over, chasing her off by killing all her hired help.

"What about your other sister?"

"Summer? No, John, she wouldn't do a thing like that. Why, she might throw things at Jerome, but she'd never kill him. No matter how he whored or got drunk, she always took him back. I think she loves him." Autumn swallowed. "Loved him," she hastily corrected.

"I suppose everyone knows he's dead now?"

"It's all over town. Do you think his killer is after you—and me?"

"A lot of people around you and your sisters end up dead."

"That's not our fault." Autumn's temper flared.

"There's no way you could ever see a three-way split of the silver coming out of the mine?"

"After what Spring did? Never!"

"Summer thinks Spring stole her husband and might even think she killed him. She must have heard about Jerome's death by now."

"Spring's husband died, too," Autumn said. "Don't you see? Any man that gets close to Spring dies. Let that be a lesson, John. You—"

Before she could continue her lecture, a sharp rap came at the door. Slocum sighed. Whatever reputation Autumn had in Tombstone was now doomed. Having a man in her room would, at the least, get her kicked out of the boardinghouse. Depending on the story the landlady spun, Autumn might as well leave town or take up residence in a cathouse. Everyone would think she was a soiled dove, or at least a woman of loose morals, for allowing a man in her room.

"Go away," Autumn said sharply.

"Want to have a word with you, Mrs. Dupree."

Slocum's hand went to his pistol just as the door opened. The marshal filled the narrow frame with his broad shoulders, but all Slocum could see was the double-barreled shotgun leveled at him.

"Don't try it, Slocum," the marshal said. "I'll blow you to hell and gone, I swear."

Slocum took his hand away from the ebony handle of his six-shooter. He had forgotten to reload. The best he could do was bluff—and the shotgun made that a losing proposition.

"What's the meaning of this? You can't barge into a lady's room and—"

"Lady?" The marshal laughed harshly. "What kind of lady has a killer in her bedroom?"

"What do you mean, Marshal?" Autumn stood her ground, but Slocum saw the lawman was inclined to shoot her, too, if it came to that.

"I mean, I got me a killer to take to the hoosegow. Come along, now. I'm arresting you for the murder of Spring Atkins."

9

"I didn't kill her," Slocum said. He considered his options and none looked good. The marshal had his finger curled around both the shotgun triggers. The slightest twitch would send enough buckshot around the room to kill a half dozen men. There wasn't any way in hell the lawman was going to miss at this range.

The marshal's eyebrows arched at Slocum's denial.

"Ain't said you were responsible. Her. I'm arresting her for the crime of murder."

Autumn gasped and put her hand to her mouth. She turned whiter than the sheets on her bed and tried to speak, but only incoherent sounds came out. Slocum was similarly shocked but recovered first.

"Mrs. Dupree wouldn't kill her own sister," he said.

"I've always heard blood's thicker'n water, but the nastiest feuds I ever did see were between brothers. Addin' in 'between sisters' ain't that much of a stretch for me. Come along, now. I got a cell all gussied up and waitin' for you."

"John, stop him. I didn't kill Spring. I saved you!"

Slocum stood stock-still as the marshal took Autumn by

the arm and steered her from the room. The marshal watched Slocum more closely than he did his prisoner, and with good reason. If the lawman had turned his back for even a split second, Slocum could have drawn his gun and laid the barrel alongside the marshal's head. One good whack would have been all it took to free Autumn. She would be on the run from the law, but Slocum could attest to the fact that being on the trail endlessly running from wanted posters was a damned sight better than being locked up in a jail cell.

Or having a noose dropped around your neck.

The commotion caused by the arrest had stirred the late-rising boarders. The landlady stood, arms crossed over her ample bosom, foot tapping in disapproval of such goings-on. When Slocum came out of Autumn's room, the landlady fixed him with a cold stare.

"You want to take her belongings with you?"

"Why would I do that? She's not going to be in jail long enough to need anything," Slocum said.

"Then she can find them out in the street. This is a respectable house. I won't tolerate such lawless behavior in my boardinghouse!"

Slocum knew better than to argue with the woman. Autumn would be released when the marshal figured out someone else had done the killing. Slocum trailed along behind the marshal and his prisoner, frowning as he thought long and hard about the matter. Killing Jerome made some sense. Summer might have done it, no matter how Autumn protested that her sister wasn't capable of such a vicious crime. If she had killed her husband, she might have killed her sister, too.

But somehow Slocum doubted that had happened. It was certainly likely that whoever had ridden into the Silver Chalice Mine and gunned down Jerome had also killed Spring, but Slocum had followed the trail of Jerome's killer until it disappeared in the desert, and he doubted that Summer Lorritsen could have laid out such a deception by herself.

If there had been anyone to take the bet, Slocum would have laid odds that someone else was trying to steal the Silver Chalice Mine. He hurried along to the jailhouse and found that the marshal had already locked Autumn into a cell. She clung to the bars and looked frantic.

"Get me out, John. Please!"

"Hush your mouth, now, Miz Dupree," the marshal said. He dropped into his desk chair and leaned back. The spindly wooden chair groaned under his bulk and provided the only other sound in the room. The Regulator clock had stopped and the other cells were as empty as a politician's promise.

"Business slow, Marshal?"

"You mean why'd I let the rest of them drunks go? I figgered the little lady might want some privacy till her trial. Got a judge willin' to hear the case tomorrow morning first thing."

"What evidence do you have that she killed Spring?"

"Got a dead body."

Slocum waited for more, but it wasn't forthcoming.

"You have a witness to Mrs. Dupree killing her sister?"

"Now, that would be tellin', wouldn't it? What's your interest in this? I heard tell you was bangin' Spring Atkins. You moved on to her sister?"

Slocum saw that the marshal was goading him intentionally. If he lost his temper, he would be in the cell next to Autumn.

"You shouldn't listen to rumors, Marshal."

"Rumors got a way of bein' true. Ain't much else to do in Tombstone but get drunk, mine silver, and gossip. Folks here do all three real good."

"Where's the body?"

"Me and a couple of my boys brung it back early this morning. It's over at the undertaker's. Good thing Miz Atkins had a pile of silver ingots from her mine to give her a decent send-off."

"Where did you find the body?"

"You surely are full of questions. Do I have to insert you into a cell to stifle them?" The marshal reached for the scattergun he had laid on his battered desk. He hardly moved, but the barrel swung around and pointed at Slocum's groin.

Slocum got the idea. He left without another word, Autumn's sobs in his ears as he stepped into the bright sun of a new Arizona day. The heat would be oppressive soon, but Slocum didn't dare let that slow him if he wanted to get Autumn free.

The undertaker's parlor was easy to find. From the look of it, he and the land office vied for the most business. Two wagons outside were loaded with bodies. One wagon had several piled up, while the other had a solitary occupant. Slocum bumped into two miners as they left.

"He's nothing less'n a road agent, that's what he is. Imagine wantin' to charge fer each of the bodies. We kin bury them out in the desert. Won't matter none to them. They're both gone to the Promised Land already."

"I dunno, Jeb. Both of the brothers wanted a Christian burial. Many's the time I heard 'em say that."

"We kin say a word over the graves. Hell and damnation, git that preacher what's always drunk and have him say a few words. He'd do damn near anything for a pint of pop skull."

The miners got into the wagon laden with the multiple bodies and rattled off amid a cloud of dust. Slocum wiped his nose as he entered. The stench outside was almost more than he could stand, and he had endured some powerful odors in his day. He waited impatiently as the undertaker dickered with another miner over the remaining body outside in the hot sun.

"We can do the special. Twelve dollars."

"That include a coffin? He'd want a pine coffin."

"Blanket for that amount," the undertaker said in a resonant, outraged tone. "A pine box adds ten dollars."

"Ain't got that much. What kind of marker does Billy get?"

"The special cross with his name carved in it. Got a young lad who'll do the carving with his pocketknife for fifty cents."

"Wood? Reckon that's all right, if his name's spelled proper. He was always goin' on 'bout how he hated it when folks spelled his name wrong, not that he could read all that good. But he knew his own name when he seen it." The miner shrugged and began counting out a handful of coins, ending with a dozen pennies when he finally reached an amount that satisfied the undertaker.

The undertaker gestured, and two somber men hardly out of their teens left with the miner to fetch Billy's body. The man turned to Slocum, put on his best solemn face, and intoned, "How may I be of service to you in your time of need?"

"Spring Atkins," Slocum said. "I want to know how she died."

The undertaker blinked once but otherwise hid any emotion.

"You are not with the marshal's office. What is your interest in Mrs. Atkins's demise?"

"The marshal claims her sister strangled Spring."

Slocum watched and got only another flicker of emotion from the undertaker. Slocum was glad he wasn't playing poker with him, because it would be a long night before he could possibly win by finding the man's tells. Slocum hoped his flat-out guess at how Spring had died would prime the pump so he could get some facts. Otherwise, he'd have to try something else.

Slocum almost cried out in relief when the undertaker corrected him.

"You are mistaken about her cause of death, sir. She was shot in the head," the man said. "From behind."

"So somebody snuck up on her and shot her when she wasn't looking? At close range?"

"Her hair was set on fire. I would say that was very close

range. The marshal saw the manner of Mrs. Atkins's death and decided a woman had done the cowardly act. He declared it must be her sister since the killing was not done face-to-face."

Slocum had to admit the marshal had jumped to a conclusion he might have himself.

"A big-caliber gun?"

"From the exit wound in her forehead, I would say it was a .44. If I might say, I am an expert in such wounds, having seen more than my share. Tombstone is not a town where many die in bed." He folded his hands on his breast and tried to conceal the tiny smile that insisted on creeping across his lips. Business was good, damned good, for a man like him in Tombstone.

There wasn't much more Slocum could get from the undertaker without forking over money for the information, so he left. The body had been removed from the wagon, which was still parked in front of the office. Of the driver who had brought Billy in, Slocum saw no trace. He looked around, then went into the nearest saloon and found the miner leaning heavily against the bar. The way he wobbled, even braced the way he was, told Slocum the man was drowning his sorrow as fast as he could knock back the shots of whiskey.

"Another one for my friend," Slocum said, indicating the grieving miner. The man looked up with bloodshot eyes.

"I know you?"

"You're taking care of Billy's burial, aren't you?"

"Yeah, but—"

"He was a good man. Hard worker. Decent miner," Slocum said, struggling to come up with something that sounded complimentary but wouldn't contradict some important fact about Billy's life.

"He was my partner for three years. We never hit it big, but we got by."

Slocum motioned for the barkeep to leave what remained in the bottle.

"You've been working a claim here for that long? Must be a decent one."

"Not that good, but good enough. Billy kept telling me we were close."

"Like at the Silver Chalice?"

The man shook his head and said, "Ain't too many mines in the region as good. Leastways not with the potential the Silver Chalice has. That crazy lady what owns it would never pay for a crew to work in the mine. Me and Billy, we offered our picks when we needed some extra money, but she wouldn't pay nuthin'. As cheap as they come, not that she couldn't git men to work for what she had to offer."

Slocum nodded. He knew what the miner meant, having experienced it firsthand.

"Was he gunned down with her? Didn't hear that, but then I've been so tore up over Billy fallin' down that shaft and bustin' his neck, a lot's passed me by."

"He died a long time back," Slocum said. "That's what I heard."

"You heard wrong. When I drove into town round dawn, I saw him over on Allen Street arguin' with one of them lawyers out in the middle of the street. Didn't pay a whole lot of attention, but from what I overheard, the lawyer wanted to hire on to stand in court for him, and he didn't want any part of it."

Slocum was out the door and headed to the Allen Street saloons in a flash. He had to get to the bottom of this because he was certain Spring had said her husband was dead. Others had said the same, but they might have only repeated what the woman had told them. He ought to have known Spring's veracity wasn't too dependable. She talked to hear her own voice and said whatever she thought the listener wanted to hear.

It took him only a few minutes to find the center of the ruckus. It was hardly mid-morning and already drunks were tumbling out of a saloon into the street. The other saloons were quiet, giving Slocum the notion this was where he wanted to be. He stepped inside. Through the heavy smoke he saw a man holding forth at a table in the center of the narrow, long room.

"It's mine, I say. I'll fight anyone to prove that. She was my wife, and what she inherited from her pa rightfully belongs to me now that she's dead."

Slocum started toward the man, then veered away when he saw two faces at the rear of the saloon he knew all too well. The two road agents who had dry-gulched him were too intent on the man spouting the nonsense about deserving the silver mine to notice Slocum, but if he sat with the braggart, they would certainly spot him. Slocum touched his Colt and remembered he still hadn't reloaded. Getting into as fight with the robbers wouldn't do him any good at the moment and would see him filled with a pound of lead.

"You, mister, what's your name?" called one road agent.

"I'm Russ Atkins, and I'm the rightful owner of the Silver Chalice Mine, that's who I am. And who the hell are you?"

"Somebody who knows sayin' you own a mine and actually ownin' it are two different things. Can you prove you own the Silver Chalice?"

"What's it to you?"

"Well, Mr. Russ Atkins, me and my partner here are interested in buyin' it. We can pay good money for it."

"Hard currency?"

"Specie," the road agent answered. This caught Slocum's attention. The robbers were talking about buying a working silver mine with their ill-gotten gains. He considered leaving town then and there to see if the two bags of silver slugs were still where he had hidden them south of town. Slocum settled his nerves. He was getting too jumpy for his own good. Of course the stolen silver was there. He hadn't told these two what he had done with their other partner's cut.

"Slow Joe," Slocum said under his breath. That was the name they had used for the robber Slocum had robbed.

"How's that?" the barkeep asked. "You with them two?"

Slocum shook his head, not wanting to speak.

"They was teamed up with a dimwit named Slow Joe. Ain't seen him in a while." The barkeep set a beer in front of Slocum, and he didn't complain. He needed something cool sliding down his gullet about now to calm him.

"Why do you suppose they're back in town?" Slocum's words came out so low the barkeep could barely hear.

"Folks die," came the simple answer. "Might be Slow Joe's one of them what died. Never had good sense in the fights he chose. Wasn't too bright teamin' up with the likes of them two. You know Clarke and Gunnison?"

"Seen them around but don't know them," Slocum said, keeping his back to the outlaws.

"They're trouble," the barkeep said before moving away, leaving Slocum to nurse the beer. In the corner of a mirror behind the bar, he caught sight of the two outlaws beside Atkins's table. This wasn't as good as watching directly, but he had to keep a low profile. More than once as the trio talked, Slocum started to leave so he could reload his six-shooter and settle accounts. Before he put the thought into action, Clarke and Gunnison left abruptly.

"I'm the owner of the richest mine in all Arizona Territory!" bellowed Atkins.

Slocum decided Clarke was right. The man boasted at the top of his lungs to convince people who otherwise could not care less about the mine's ownership. Picking up his beer, Slocum went to the table and sat down.

"I didn't invite you to join me."

"A rich man like you ought to be nice to the riffraff," Slocum said caustically. Atkins didn't notice the tone.

"I'm in mourning. You got to excuse me."

"Mourning? For Spring?" Slocum saw how Atkins stiffened and moved his hand toward a pocket in his brocade vest. The outline of a derringer told the reason for the slight shift. "She said you were dead."

"She only wished I was dead. The bitch would hop into bed with anybody and I got fed up, so I left her."

Slocum doubted that. The lure of both silver and even an occasional roll in the hay with a woman like Spring would have kept Russ Atkins sniffing around, no matter what. Slocum didn't see that the man had the pride necessary to actually leave, even if Spring tried to dictate every instant of his behavior.

"But you came back."

"Too late to save her from her own sister. Autumn is a heartless bitch. Shot her down without so much as a fare-thee-well. Now it's up to me to get what I can out of the Silver Chalice. In her memory, of course. Why, those two gents that just left wanted to buy the mine. You in the market, mister?"

"Might be," Slocum said. "Folks around here know you? From before you left Spring?"

"What are you saying?" Fingers pressed into the derringer now. It wouldn't take much more to goad Atkins into taking a shot at him. Slocum softened his tone a little. His own empty six-gun provided a constant reminder of the trouble he could find himself in if he wasn't careful.

"Might be we can work together," Slocum said. "I've been out to the mine."

"You mean you and Sp—"

"That, too," Slocum said, making a dismissive motion with his hand. "There's a powerful lot of silver chloride ore in that mine."

"What are you offering? To work the mine? You don't look like a miner to me. From the way you're dressed, you sure as hell can't buy it. That's what I want. To find a buyer. It's a fitting memorial for her."

"I reckon not a whole lot of people in town remember you when Spring was still alive. Might be I can jog their memories, drop a hint here and there about how we got drunk together. How you are her husband. Would that give you an edge in securing your claim to the mine—and selling it?" Slocum had no idea if this gent was Spring's husband, but selling the mine rather than working it was his obvious goal.

Slocum thought he was past being surprised. Russ Atkins exploded in anger.

"I don't need nobody lyin' about me. I never laid eyes on you before, and I sure as hell don't need you vouchin' for me. I'm Spring's husband and the Silver Chalice is my inheritance!"

Slocum had expected the man to take him up on the offer—and that would have meant he was an impostor. By getting angry and turning Slocum down, he had shown he had a decent claim on the mine.

"No offense," Slocum said, standing and backing away. He left the saloon and entered the furnace of another Arizona Territory day. The three sisters had never played straight, so he had assumed a man claiming to be one of their husbands wouldn't either.

Slocum had been moved toward thinking Russ Atkins actually was Spring's husband. He shook his head. Finding a way to get Autumn out of jail had gotten harder. Atkins wasn't likely to stop telling anyone who'd listen that not only was he the rightful heir but that Spring's sister was the killer.

Atkins's legitimate claim meant he was most likely to have killed the woman, since he had the most to gain from her death.

How did Slocum prove it? There didn't seem to be a way. As he walked, he reloaded his six-shooter and felt better for it, even if he didn't have anyone in his sights to shoot.

Yet.

10

"There might be something in it for you," Clarke said to the land clerk. Slocum watched through an open window and read what the outlaw didn't. The clerk wasn't going to be bribed, at least not by anything Clarke offered.

"I don't lose land deeds," the clerk said. "That wouldn't be . . . efficient."

"Well, then," Clarke said, getting red in the face. "Maybe this whole damned office might burn down, with the records and the clerk inside. It might take a long time for the volunteer fire department to sober up and get here."

"You know Judge Watkins?"

"What's that got to do with anything?" Clarke demanded. He motioned and Gunnison came to stand beside him. Slocum had to admit they presented an imposing front to the slight, bespectacled clerk. For his part, though, the clerk never backed down.

"Got 'bout everything to do with it. You ought to take lessons from him about scarin' the bejesus out of people. He scares me. You don't." The clerk reached under the counter and pulled out a sawed-off shotgun. "I got this loaded with carpet tacks. Don't make it too accurate, but at this range, I'd spatter most of your guts—both of your bellies—against the far wall. I'd rather clean that up than have Judge Watkins find I'd forged a land deed."

"We'll be back."

"Don't come back 'less you got a legit claim to file. I don't have the time for peg boys like you two."

"You son of a bitch!" Gunnison smashed into the counter and grabbed for the clerk. Again Slocum found himself surprised at the outcome. The clerk swung the short-barreled weapon around hard into Gunnison's wrist. A loud crunch was instantly followed by the man's screech of pain. Then even that vanished as the clerk swung the butt of the shotgun around and drove it smack into the middle of Gunnison's forehead. The man fell facedown onto the counter.

"Get him out of here. I've got a real customer comin' in."

Clarke snarled and shook his partner hard. When this didn't bring him around, Clarke grabbed his collar and dragged him from the land office. The clerk waited for them to close the door before returning his weapon to its spot under the counter.

Over his shoulder, he called out, "You come on in and let's talk. Less you're one of them Peeping Toms, and there's not a whole lot I've got you'd want to stare at."

Slocum laughed and came around, being sure Clarke and Gunnison were nowhere near. He went in and put his hands on the counter to show the clerk he wasn't going to make the same mistake Gunnison had.

"Not much gets by you, does it?"

"I run this here town," the clerk said. "That's not an exaggeration. The politicians and lawyers and lawmen think they do, but what I say goes. Now, other than givin' you a stage show, what can I do for you?"

"I wanted to look at the deed for the Silver Chalice."

"Public record. No reason why you can't get a gander at

it," the clerk said, but he made no move to get the records book. Slocum dropped a silver dollar on the counter, then followed it with another when the clerk simply stared at him. The man nodded once and fetched the thick book. He hummed to himself and finally found the page. He opened the book, turned it around for Slocum, and said, "This is the deed, attested to and duly recorded by yours truly."

The clerk didn't budge, but Slocum didn't care. He read quickly down the deed and saw that Spring had recorded the mine solely in her name. Women couldn't own real estate, so this strengthened Russ Atkins's claim to the mine. Or did it?

He looked up, but the clerk answered before he could pose the question.

"He's got to prove they were married when she filed. If a local judge performed the ceremony or one of the preachers in town, that shouldn't be hard. Otherwise, a jury might have to decide who owns the Silver Chalice. I hope not, since that means I'd have to close the office while I testified as an expert witness."

"Could her sister inherit?"

"Same problem. Women can't own real estate, but there's nothing that says she couldn't inherit it, then sell it. This here mine's 'bout the best around out east of town. Certainly as good as anything Ed Schieffelin found, and he's the standard around here. Now, the Good Enough Mine is likely to produce more, but them boys are goin' at it as a business, not a hobby. They prob'ly got twenty or more miners working it."

Slocum pushed the records book back. He noticed that when the clerk hefted it and put it back in its place the two silver dollars were gone, as if by magic. Slocum left, again warily looking around to be sure he didn't run into Clarke and Gunnison. The time would come when he was ready, but dealing with Autumn's imprisonment required his full attention right now. When he finished with the two outlaws, he'd likely have to leave town in a hurry, the law on his trail.

He kept in the shade as much as he could as he approached the courthouse along Toughnut Street. The imposing two-story structure had a pair of armed men sitting on the front step. As he neared, he saw the glint of sunlight off their badges. One shifted the rifle in the crook of his arm as Slocum neared. Slocum touched the brim of his hat and said, "Good afternoon."

The man grunted a reply but never stopped watching Slocum all the way into the courthouse. Slocum looked around when he reached the lobby and then cocked his head to one side when he heard a familiar, too-loud voice echoing from a court bailiff's office. He stepped closer and chanced a quick look inside.

Russ Atkins leaned over a desk, his hands balled into fists. The muttonchop bewhiskered man seated behind the desk didn't appear too intimidated by the man's belligerence. The public officials in Tombstone had seen it all, heard it all, and had passed being easily intimidated by the likes of Atkins—or the two outlaws.

"You have to present this to the judge for me. You have to!"

"Mr. Atkins, matters like this take a spell. We got a full docket, and probate on a will isn't much of a priority."

"You put things on the docket for the judge, don't you?"

"That's my job, as well as keeping order in the court and occasionally sweeping up around the courthouse if I can't find a young'un to do it. You might say I'm a jack of all trades entrusted with keeping proper order in all matters."

"I can't work the mine until this is settled. Might be I could use a silent partner in the mine."

"How silent?"

"Not so silent that he wouldn't speak up now and then, when business was called for."

"Such as scheduling a probate?"

"Five percent."

"Ten," the bailiff said without an instant's hesitation.

Russ Atkins reached across the desk and shook the man's hand. Slocum took this as his cue to slip out the door and back into the desert heat. For all his bluster, Atkins knew how to move things along. He had to be pretty sure of himself to force the matter into court, where any hint of forgery would see the Silver Chalice Mine seized by the county. Only the politicians and lawyers would profit from that, but Atkins showed no fear of that happening.

Slocum went back down the street, up Fourth Street, and wound his way through the maze of streets until he eventually got to the jailhouse.

"John!" Autumn leaped to her feet and clung to the bars when he stepped inside. She had been crying. The dusty tracks down her cheeks gave mute testimony to her fear and sorrow.

"You hold it, mister," said the deputy sitting at the marshal's desk reading a penny dreadful. "No visitors. Them's my orders."

"You or her?" Slocum asked. The question confused the deputy for a moment.

"Her, I reckon. Why'd the marshal not want me to have any visitors?"

"Can't say since you're such a friendly looking cuss," Slocum said, pulling up a chair to face the deputy. "But it's you I've come to see."

"Why me?"

"I wanted to let you know about Spring Atkins's husband. Russ has been going around town trying to get himself declared legal heir to the mine. He wants to sell it as soon as he gets title free and clear."

"No foolin'?" the deputy said, puzzled. Slocum saw Autumn taking this all in as he had hoped she would.

"He's bribed the court bailiff to put the probate of a will on the docket right away."

"Will? Spring had a will?" Autumn couldn't help speaking out.

"You hush up," the deputy said, glaring at Autumn. To Slocum he said, "I don't know about no will."

"Spring told me he was dead, so why'd she mention him in her will, if there even is one?"

"I'd heard he was dead, too," the deputy said. "But not from Maude. Maybe if she'd tole me he was dead, it woulda been the truth. She's got her ear to the ground better'n anybody else in this here town."

"I'm going to poke around the Silver Chalice and see what I can find. Might be I can find a forged will from Spring's pa."

"What are you goin' on about, mister?" The deputy scowled. "I don't know what you're sayin'."

"If Spring wasn't entitled to inherit the mine from her pa, then Russ Atkins isn't the one who should inherit it at all."

"Thank you, John!" Autumn mouthed. He flashed her a quick smile, then stood.

"Been good talking to you," he said to the deputy. Slocum left the young man scratching his head, wondering what was going on.

Slocum stood out in the sun, wondering what to do. He needed evidence and had nowhere to turn for it. The bailiff might be forced to confess he had accepted a bribe from Russ Atkins, but the bribe had been for an insignificant crime. Slocum wasn't even sure it was a crime for the bailiff to use his authority to change the order of court cases. Worse, the bailiff could make the claim that Atkins was paying court costs for probate, not bribing him.

Autumn was accused of murder, not trivial crimes such as Atkins had committed. Slocum needed to find Spring's killer to free Autumn. As he walked, dust kicking up around his boots and forming small dust devils, he worked through all that had happened at the mine. No matter how he considered it, Autumn didn't seem to be the murderer. A large-caliber pistol had been used by someone sneaking up behind Spring. If the killing had been done in the heat of the moment—two sisters arguing—Spring would have been shot in the chest or face.

Slocum should have asked the undertaker where Spring's body had been discovered. He'd bet the bags of silver slugs he had taken from Slow Joe that she hadn't been at the mine. For all he knew, she had been in town. He had been pinned down in the mine for some time. She might have been killed while he was being shot at. While that didn't clear Autumn, it didn't condemn her, either. If she had killed Spring, all she had to do was walk up and repeat the murder with Slocum. She had risked her life to get him safely away from the sniper.

The bushwhacker had been intent on murder. Slocum rubbed the back of his head where he had banged it on the floor of the mine. The dull ache was fading, but the memory of how helpless he had been trapped inside without a six-shooter remained to haunt him.

It made no sense for Autumn to kill her sister, then go through a charade of saving Slocum. The marshal hadn't tried to pin the murder on anyone but Autumn.

Slocum slowed and then moved to the shade of a cottonwood along the street when he saw Russ Atkins talking earnestly with a man dressed as a miner. While he might be recruiting workers for when the Silver Chalice was his free and clear, it didn't look that way to Slocum. The miner held out his hand and a sheaf of greenbacks changed hands. The miner didn't bother to count them. He stuffed them into his shirt pocket, then shook with Atkins.

Atkins hurried away, mounted his horse, and rode hard from town in the direction of the mine.

Slocum considered following the man, then decided to see what so much money had bought. The miner went into the Birdcage Saloon and had a couple stiff jolts of whiskey.

He had the look of a man who could put away an entire bottle and only then get woozy, but he turned down the barkeep when asked about a third drink. The miner looked repeatedly at a large clock ticking quietly at the rear of the saloon, near the steps leading up to the theater balcony.

With sudden resolve, the miner left the saloon. Slocum wasn't surprised when the man strode past other saloons, never giving them a look. He didn't even respond when a whore in a second-story window called down lewd suggestions. Slocum had seen men on a mission; the miner had become single-minded in whatever task lay ahead.

Curious, Slocum trailed him to a gunsmith. A few minutes after entering the shop, the miner emerged with a heavy six-shooter thrust into his belt. The man didn't look entirely comfortable with the hogleg, but Slocum was beginning to think marksmanship wasn't what he had been paid for.

Slocum walked faster, closing the gap between him and the miner. The man's destination was apparent now. The Tombstone jail was ahead and might as well have had a giant X painted on its wall. The miner went there and nowhere else.

He looked around guiltily, then ducked down the alley behind the jail. Slocum ran now to get to the corner of the jailhouse. The man dragged a crate over to a spot under the barred cell window and climbed up. He slid the six-gun from his belt and lifted it to the window.

Slocum had already figured out this was Autumn's cell.

He drew his Colt in a smooth movement, stepped around the corner of the jail, and took aim at the miner's head. The sudden movement spooked the man. He turned, lost his balance on the crate, stumbled, and fell heavily. The six-shooter flew from his hand.

"Don't reach for it," Slocum said coldly. He aimed directly at the miner's face. A slight pressure on the trigger would send a round through the man's brain. Slocum remembered the last time he had been in a position like this. Autumn had prevented him from killing Winthrop. Only that memory caused him to keep from drawing back and loosing a round.

"Why did Atkins pay you to kill her?"

"Wh-what are you talking about? I'm not going to kill anybody!"

"The woman in the cell." Slocum didn't point. He held his pistol in a rock-steady grip aimed at the miner. "You were paid to kill her."

"No, mister, no! That's not why I got all the money. H-here, you can have it. Take it all!" The miner fumbled and pulled out the wad of greenbacks thick enough to choke a cow. He held it out to Slocum as if it were some sort of religious offering.

"I saw you poke the gun through the bars. You were going to kill her."

"I was paid to slip her the gun so she could escape!"

Slocum's aim wavered and gave the miner the chance to roll onto his hands and knees, then get some traction by digging his toes into the hard, sun-baked ground and run away as fast as his short legs could carry him.

Slocum raised his pistol, got the man in his sights, then lowered his gun. He slid it back into his holster. He hefted the six-gun the miner had dropped and thrust it into his belt. He took a few minutes to gather the greenbacks scattered around.

At least the man had been able to buy himself a couple shots of whiskey.

Slocum pieced it together as appreciation came to him for how subtle Atkins had been. The miner had been paid to get the six-shooter and slip it to Autumn so she could shoot her way out of the cell. If she got away, she'd be branded as her sister's killer. She might even wound or kill a deputy during the escape. So much the better from Atkins's viewpoint.

And if Autumn were killed, this was the best of all outcomes for Russ Atkins. His wife's death would be written off as solved, and possible legal tangles with Autumn asking for the mine would be removed. Slocum doubted Atkins knew of the forged will Spring had used to get the mine, but even if this surfaced, it wouldn't mean anything. Autumn would still be branded as her sister's killer.

Slocum considered breaking Autumn out of the jail. The two of them could ride off. He had plenty of money from the desert robbery. A bag of silver planchet would keep them in style for quite a spell. Even as the notion came to him, he forgot about it. Clearing Autumn was the only sensible thing to do. She might not cotton much to riding with a man who had stolen silver coins from a robber. She certainly wouldn't want a murder indictment following her wherever she rode.

He retrieved his horse and rode eastward, on Russ Atkins's trail. Spring's husband had only one thing on his mind and that was the Silver Chalice. Slocum cut across country to shave a few miles' ride off the trip and arrive ahead of Atkins.

Slocum left his horse down the arroyo he and Autumn had used to get away before and approached the camp on foot. He slid the heavier six-shooter from his belt, keeping his own Colt in reserve. A quick look through the cabin window showed no one inside. Slocum entered and began his search for the bogus will Spring had used to gain the Silver Chalice Mine after her pa died.

Hunt as he might, he couldn't find the will that would prove Russ Atkins had no claim to the mine—at least, not through inheriting his wife's belongings.

When he heard a horse neigh, Slocum abandoned his search and slipped from the cabin. It had to be Atkins who had come to the mine, but Slocum couldn't figure out where the man was. Movement at the mouth of the mine warned him someone had just entered.

A slow smile came to his lips. He had been trapped before in the mine, pinned down by a gunman outside. It was his turn now to gain the upper hand. He'd learn everything he could from Atkins and then turn him over to the marshal. Showing up on the heels of his wife's murder was a mite too convenient, and Slocum was sure Atkins had a part in killing Spring.

He walked briskly to the mouth of the mine, then got a sinking feeling that he had made a terrible mistake. From the corner of his eye he saw two horses.

Beside the horses stood Clarke, who spotted Slocum at the same instant that Slocum recognized him. He yelled for Gunnison, who ran from the mine.

"It's Slocum!" Clarke warned his partner.

Gunnison's reply was drowned out when both men started firing. Lead flew all around, forcing Slocum down. He had to take cover, but Clarke cut off retreat back to the cabin. Gunnison threw enough lead in his direction that Slocum saw only one place where he could take cover.

He ran for the mine. The difference this time was that he had two six-shooters and doubted the outlaws would make a lengthy fight of it. They were cowards and would run once he got down to serious shooting.

Slocum ducked into the mine, skidded to a halt, and took a deep whiff. He coughed. The smell of burning fuse was distinctive. As his eyes adjusted to the dim light, he saw the sputtering fuse and the dynamite attached to the other end.

He tried to run from the cave, but the outlaws' bullets drove him back.

Then the explosion lifted him and shoved him deeper into the mine before collapsing the roof and leaving him in dusty, choking darkness.

11

Slocum coughed and forced himself to his hands and knees. Getting up from here was harder since he had a ton of rock on his back, or so it seemed. The grit in his mouth carried a tang of blood with it, and all he heard was a distant ringing. That remnants of the explosion died down as Slocum shook himself like a wet dog, sending stone fragments and dust in all directions. He twisted around and sat with his back against a rocky wall. He had to blink a few times to convince himself he wasn't blind. He knew he wasn't dead, unless this was hell and he was doomed for eternity to ache in every bone.

He coughed out blood and dirt as he forced himself to stand. When he bumped his head against the mine roof, he knew he wasn't in too bad trouble. If the mine roof had collapsed, he would have been crushed flatter than a stink-bug under a boot heel.

Fumbling about, he found the metal box in his vest pocket and pulled out the lucifers. He worked carefully to avoid losing them in the dark. The sudden flare blinded him, and the sulfur fumes from the match caused him to cough up more blood and grime again. He held the smoking match up and got a quick look at the trouble he found himself in. The outlaws had dynamited the mouth of the mine, so he wasn't too far from breathing hot desert air again. The problem lay in how much rock had been brought down by the stick or two Gunnison had used.

If either he or Clarke had been more knowledgeable, they could have collapsed the Silver Chalice all the way back with only a few sticks of explosive. That they had simply tossed it into the first crevice they found told him they didn't know a thing about mining or blasting. The match sputtered out. Slocum waited a few minutes before lighting another so he could move closer to the rock plug and use the light to better advantage.

He hunted for any glimmer of light in the rock fall but found nothing to cheer him. His earlier inspection of the mine told him there wasn't a safety vent anywhere to climb out. Spring and probably her pa before her had been interested more in the amount of silver chloride they could yank out of the mine rather than the miners' safety. Time lost putting in an escape hole was time lost digging for more ore.

Slocum had a half dozen lucifers left, but he tucked them away in his pocket for later. He needed to find a few miner's candles before using another of the precious light sources. Edging around in the dark might have taken him a minute or an hour. He lost all track of anything but careful touching and reaching for the candles. When he finally found a shelf of them, he used another match and discovered he had gone almost fifty feet deeper into the mine. His first foray into the mine had missed these entirely.

He sat and reflected on what to do. He had eight candles, good for about that many hours. Digging out would be difficult, but the sooner he started the sooner he'd be free. He doubted Clarke and Gunnison were waiting around outside. Their job had been to seal the mine and make it worthless to Russ Atkins so he would sell. That was the only reason Slocum could come up with for the detonation.

They reckoned Atkins wanted a quick buck and not a life-time of hard work, so he would sell to them. They could open the mine again at their leisure.

They had come upon a scheme to explain where they'd gotten so much silver and to spend it freely. They could present the silver slugs as being from the mine; everybody knew this was a valuable property. When they reached the end of the silver, they could either open the Silver Chalice again and make an honest living as miners—which Slocum doubted would happen—or sell it to someone else. After all, it had been producing a lot of high-grade silver.

Slocum grudgingly admired the outlaws' scheme, if that's what it was. He'd gladly do what he could to stop it, espe-cially if it meant a chance to steal the portion of the silver shipment he hadn't already taken from Slow Joe, but he had to get out of the mine first. The thick wall of rock keeping him away from freedom was too daunting for words.

He began working steadily, taking rocks from the top of the cave-in and tossing them behind him into the mine. He couldn't help noticing after the third hour that the rocks he tossed back contained fairly high-grade ore. The Silver Chal-ice was more than a dodge to put into circulation stolen silver slugs. A man working this mine could get mighty rich.

When his seventh candle flickered out, forcing him to light the eighth and final one, Slocum realized that a man inside this mine could get mighty dead, too. The air seemed stuffier to him, although he knew there was no way he could have burned up or breathed in that much in only seven hours. The Silver Chalice went far into the mountain-side and had more air than he could use.

"Use in a lifetime," he muttered. His lips were chapped, and his tongue felt bigger than a cow's. The aches he had accumulated during the explosion had turned into fire every time he moved. But he kept moving, and kept moving rock, and fed the notion he was going to get out of the mine alive.

By the time the last candle sputtered and was about ready

to extinguish itself permanently, he pushed hard and a rock rolled away. It took him a few seconds to realize what that meant. The rock rolled away. Down the far side of the cave-in!

Cold air gusted through the hole and evaporated sweat on his forehead. He basked in the breeze, then panicked. He thought he had bored his way through, but he saw nothing. Darkness.

Slocum reined in his emotions. He had burrowed through. It had taken him so long that it was nighttime. That explained the cool air. The desert turned freezing fast once the sun set. He lay forward on the pile, face in the wind, recovering his strength. His head felt as if it would split apart, and his mouth was nothing but a cotton bale. He needed water bad, but the only way to get it was to keep digging.

He dug in the dark. He kept digging, occasionally collapsing and passing out, only to shake himself awake again to keep clawing at the rock until sunlight greeted him.

The hole was still too small for him to wiggle through. The problem was that a huge rock had fallen from the roof and had been followed by the looser stones he had pawed his way through. The huge rock beneath was as impenetrable to his bloodied fingers as the cavity above from which it had fallen. He could get air and sunlight, but escape seemed forever denied him. The Silver Chalice was going to be his grave.

"Silver coffin," he muttered. He laughed louder at the crazy notion. "I'm gonna have a silver coffin. Never thought I'd do better than pinewood. Silver coffin, all around me, millions of dollars in silver."

"That's a strange request."

"Not a request. That's what happened." Slocum forced his eyelids to rise. He squinted against the sun, then didn't have to, as someone came between him and the bright light.

"How do I get you out of there, John?"

"Autumn?"

"Who else would you expect?"

"You're in jail. In Tombstone."

"And you're caged in my silver mine."

"Can you dig me out? There's a huge rock, too big, can't move it or go round it." The first flare of energy at hearing the woman's voice had faded now, leaving him as exhausted as before.

"It's not a natural cave-in, so somebody blew it up."

"Clarke and Gunnison."

"Do they work for my brother-in-law?"

"I doubt it. I followed Atkins and thought he was coming here. Turned out the two sidewinders had plans of their own, and I don't think Atkins had anything to do with them."

"That's a surprise. He's been sucking up to every lowlife in Tombstone trying to sell them this mine."

"Water," Slocum croaked.

"Oh, yes, sorry. Here." Slocum saw a hand moving as she held up a canteen, but the water wasn't going to reach him through the narrow hole he had opened.

"I can't even get a tin cup through," Autumn said. "Let me try something else."

Slocum pressed his cheek against the rock, half lost in a coma. Then he felt something wet moving against his forehead. He looked up to see Autumn stuffing a rope through the narrow hole.

"I've soaked it in water. Wring it out."

"Not enough. Rope's not wet enough. Cloth," he said. "Soak some cloth and I can pull it through."

"A good idea."

He heard ripping sounds and sloshing. A tug on the rope told him he could pull the soaked rag through. When he got it past the last of the rock, he opened his mouth and squeezed as hard as he could. He was surprised at how weak his grip was, but the dribble of water rejuvenated him. Doing this repeatedly helped take the edge off his thirst—he still needed more—but he was thinking clearer now.

"The only way I can get out is to dynamite the opening again. Have you ever used dynamite?"

"Can't say that I have," Autumn said slowly. "I can poke it all through to you and—"

"No," Slocum cut in. "The blast would kill me. Go back down the mine tunnel. You're going to have to plant the charge outside."

"Well, all right, but you'll owe me for this. Especially if I blow myself up."

"If you do that, we'll both be together in the Promised Land," Slocum said.

"You have a mighty high opinion of yourself."

Slocum had to laugh.

"Let's not worry about that until we get there." He explained how to crimp the fuse onto the blasting cap and how to light it.

"I might blow my head off. Can't I do it some other way than biting down on it?"

"Find the dynamite and fuse. There might be a crimping tool there with the caps."

She disappeared. Slocum almost called out to her not to go, but he held back his irrational demand. If Autumn didn't find the dynamite, she'd have to go for help. He wasn't sure who in Tombstone would be amenable to helping out, even if she asked nicely.

"There," she said. "I've done everything you said. It's ready to blow. Or light or whatever."

"Put the charge about halfway up the fallen block. Look for a crack. Stick it there."

"Sounds more exciting if you weren't talking about rocks and dynamite."

The woman's words took him aback. Then he laughed again. He was getting giddy from the lack of water and food. Autumn had seemed so prim and proper, he had to be misunderstanding her words.

"There's a large crevice to one side of the block."

"It has to be on the block. Toward the top?"

"I can barely squeeze in two sticks."

"Do it. Light the fuse and run. How long did you give yourself?"

"Two feet equaled two minutes, you said. I can be on the far side of the cabin."

"Good."

"Good luck, John. See you on this side of the mine in a couple minutes."

Before he could answer, he heard the hissing fuse as it began burning. He slid back down the rocky slope and stumbled deeper into the mine, until the sun looked as if it came through hardly more than a pinhole. Then the earth shook and he fell to his knees. The blast didn't deafen him this time, but the dust was choking. The shock lifted dirt from the floor and dust from the walls and ceiling, making an impenetrable cloud.

Slocum pulled up his bandanna to cover his nose and mouth. Waving his arm to clear the air, he made his way forward. He saw Autumn waving to him from the other side of a goodly sized hole blown through the block. He flopped on his belly and wiggled through, not caring if he cut up his chest in his haste to get out of the Silver Chalice.

The instant he reached the freedom of the hot Arizona sun, he found himself engulfed in arms and smothered with kisses.

"You got out. I did it right. You weren't killed."

"Whoa," he said. "I need some air."

Autumn laughed in delight, pushed away from him, and held out a canteen. He tried not to seem too greedy when he pulled the cork and began drinking. It was only warm water, but nothing had ever tasted finer. He slowed his gulping and let some of the water slosh on his face. Autumn giggled now.

"You look like a clay statue." She hugged him again and buried her cheek in his dusty chest. "I thought you were a goner."

"How'd you get out of jail?" Slocum looked around. If either Clarke or Gunnison was still here, they'd have opened fire by now. Still, he was spooked by getting trapped in the mine.

"I finally persuaded Judge Alvarcz to let me go. It, uh, took a while, but he was . . . persuaded." She spat the words out. Tombstone was a town where anything could be bought with enough silver—or sex.

"How'd you come to save me?"

"I heard a couple men in the courthouse talking about Russ and the claim. I knew you would come here since you did so much to help clear my name. The judge told me enough so I could guess the rest. You're the best there is, John. The utter best." She hugged him again.

"Let's get out of the sun. It's strange, but I went a long time without much light, and now that I'm bathed in it, I want to get out of it again."

"The cabin," Autumn said. Something in her tone set Slocum's pulse racing a little faster.

They went to her sister's cabin. The coolness revitalized Slocum almost as much as the water. He glanced at the mussed-up bed and remembered how he and Spring had—

His memory turned instantly to the present. Autumn reached around him from behind and unfastened his gunbelt and let it drop to the floor. He started to protest and then felt her hands pressing into his groin.

"Something's growing there," Autumn whispered hotly in his ear before she began nibbling on the lobe. Slocum's heart pounded so loud he wondered if she could hear it.

Her tongue slid into his ear and then down. She recoiled and laughed, but her groping fingers never left his crotch.

"I got a mouthful of dirt."

"You ought to have a mouthful of something else," he said.

"That's what I was thinking." Autumn's quick fingers unfastened his jeans, opening his fly one button at a time.

She skinned him out of his pants and then moved around in front of him. Her bright eyes glowed, and then she concentrated on the fleshy stalk growing from his crotch. Her lips took the purpled tip as her cheeks went hollow. She sucked harder and harder. As her tongue began working on the sensitive underside of his manhood, Slocum went weak in the knees. He had been through so much in the past day he couldn't stand any more.

But he could stand her mouth working on him until hell froze over.

Slocum sank down to the bed and leaned back. Autumn hungrily swarmed up and kept kissing, licking, and sucking on him until he was harder than a steel bar.

"I want you," she said, looking up. "This is nice, but I want more from you. I want to reward you for everything you've done for me."

She backed away, got to her feet, and did a slow striptease for him. He did the impossible. He got even harder watching as her snowy breasts were revealed when her blouse fell away. She worked at the fastener on her skirt and finally released it. The skirt dropped to the ground. She wasn't wearing anything underneath.

Autumn stepped forward, put her knees on either side of his hips, and lowered herself onto him. He sank slowly into her heated depths. For a moment they were both suspended in a bubble of timelessness. Slocum watched as Autumn seemed frozen above him. Her breasts bobbed about gently, but her expression was fixed and her hips did not move. He was buried entirely within her moist core.

Then a shudder passed through her. She tightened down around him and began massaging his length without using her hands. He gasped as white-hot lust built within his balls.

He reached up and fondled her breasts. This got her moving. Slowly at first and then with greater speed, she rose and fell on his fleshy pole, twisting this way and that as she traveled up and down. Her hands pressed into the backs of Slocum's to keep them on her breasts. Then Autumn rocked back until Slocum thought she would break him off inside her.

"So good, so damned good," she gasped out. "I want more."

Slocum got his hands around her body and cupped her buttocks. Squeezing there, kneading like he held two lumps of bread dough, pushed her arousal even higher. He half sat up and kissed her. All the while she kept moving. The desire within Slocum mounted until he was sure he would melt. Never in the hot desert sun had he felt such heat.

His arms worked to the small of her back, and he twisted around, supporting her, keeping her around him, him in her, her female sheath around him, until she lay on the bed and he was between her legs. One foot on the floor for leverage, he began thrusting powerfully. Autumn gasped and moaned and strained under him. She wanted more. He gave it to her.

She arched her back and rammed her hips up hard into him as she let out a cry that was more animal than human. When he could no longer restrain himself, he thrust mightily as if trying to split her apart. The lava within exploded outward, and he gasped. He felt her shudder again in release and then he sank onto her. They had built up quite a sweat with the heat, both desert and sexual, and mud was caking them together.

"We need a bath," he said. "Sorry about that."

"I'm not," Autumn said in a dreamy voice. She stretched like a contented cat. "The bath doesn't sound like a bad idea, but I have a better one."

"What's that?"

It took a while for him to respond again, but she showed him.

12

"Just because a judge let you out doesn't mean you're in the clear," Slocum pointed out. He stretched aching joints. Sleeping on the narrow bed would have been difficult enough, but with Autumn in his arms all night, he had cramped up muscles that might never unwind.

"I've got it all worked out, John," she said, sitting on the edge of the bed and carefully buttoning up her shoe. "I spent the last year in Tombstone listening and learning. There isn't a whole lot that's gone on in town I don't know about. You wouldn't believe what lawyers and whores and miners will do."

"I'd believe it," Slocum said. His thoughts wandered. He saw no point in returning to Tombstone other than to get even with Clarke and Gunnison. Those two sidewinders needed their heads cut off. While the explosion hadn't been intended to trap him in the Silver Chalice, it had. And the outlaws had not been too inclined to get him out. He imagined they'd returned to Tombstone and celebrated both making the mine worthless without a passel of work to reopen it and giving him a rocky grave.

"I want this mine, John. I blew open a big enough hole for a miner to get through. That means I can dig out the silver and pay for the rest of the work. I intend to be rich. Spring stole this mine from me as surely as the sun comes up over the mountains every morning."

"Her husband looks to have the inside track on bribes."

"I got a bigger judge on my side."

"Might be, but Atkins is not going to give up easily. I thought he was coming out here when I followed him from town. I don't have any notion where he really went."

"He hired those two owlhoots," she said, as if trying on the story. "He hired Clarke and Gunnison to blow up the mine to make it look like too much work to reopen, but I—we—know what it's really worth. It is only going to slow me down, not stop me."

"The explosion hurts Atkins more than you. If he was able to pull some silver from the mine, he could use it for his legal work. Offer enough money and you can choose the best lawyer in town." Slocum opened the cabin door. The heat had already built and the sun was hardly moving up in the sky. It was going to be a long, hot ride no matter where he went.

"This does cut him off from using the Silver Chalice to finance his scheme," Autumn said. "Good."

"It might also be a trick to win some sympathy. If it looks like somebody's trying to keep him out of the mine, it might strengthen his case. Or maybe he can sell it faster to somebody willing to open it up. He wouldn't get as much, but Atkins didn't look like the patient kind to me."

She sidled up behind Slocum and put her arms around his waist as she pressed her cheek against his back.

"I need you, John. Don't leave me. I know that's what you've been thinking. Me and you, this mine, we can team up and be rich. Spring's crook husband can't stop us if we stick together."

"I don't know what I'd do with my saddlebags crammed

with greenbacks," he said. But he did know. The silver slugs from the robbery buried south of town would keep him in fine style for a long time.

"You're a restless man. I know that. Just don't go riding away for a while longer. Help me. Then you can leave. No strings. Ride on when I can give you those saddlebags."

It was a tempting offer, and Slocum admitted to himself he wasn't inclined to leave Autumn behind. Besides, he had a pair of varmints to bring down. With a little luck, he could claim their portion of the silver from the robbery and not take so much as an ounce of the metal from Autumn. After what she had been through, she ought to keep everything from the Silver Chalice. She deserved that and so much more.

"I'll see you back to town. We can talk more then," he said.

"I knew you'd see it my way." She spun him around and kissed him hard, then drew back and looked up at him. The smile on her lips showed how perfectly satisfied she was with herself. "Let's saddle up and ride. I don't want to be out in the desert in the middle of the worst part of the day."

Slocum made a point of filling the canteen Autumn had given him the day before as well as his own so they would have plenty for the trip.

Even with such a delightful riding companion and plenty of water, Slocum was worn to a frazzle by the time they reached Tombstone. The sun sank in the distance, shining into his eyes and forcing him to pull down the brim of his hat. The last thing he wanted to do was ride down Fremont Street and spot Clarke or Gunnison waiting to shoot him down. But he knew this was not going to happen. They thought they had sealed him up forever in the mine shaft.

"You go on and get a drink or two, John," Autumn said. "I have a judge to see and some court orders to get issued."

"You make it sound easy."

"Oh, it will be. Like I said, I've spent the last year learning where all the skeletons are hidden. It's time for me to do some bone rattling." She laughed and rode closer. She boldly reached over and gripped his pommel. "After this is done, you can do all the bone rattling you want." She swung back and put her heels to the horse's flanks and trotted away.

Slocum watched her ride off with a curious sense of foreboding. Autumn thought getting clear title to the mine was going to be easy. He doubted it would happen without a real fight, certainly in court and probably outside the courtroom as well. Russ Atkins wasn't the kind of man to give in or give up.

Before he could decide whether Autumn needed his help, she turned down Fifth Street and disappeared. He licked his lips and considered her recommendation of a shot or two of whiskey. Water all day was fine, but a touch of tarantula juice would revitalize him. Since it didn't much matter which watering hole he chose, he drew rein and stepped down in front of a saloon that shared the side wall with the post office and had draped a tarp down at an angle to hold back the sun. The bar was set up on a plank held up by two sawhorses.

The dozen bottles of booze on a crate behind the barkeep looked good enough to drink. So he decided he would.

"I've got a big thirst," Slocum said. "What'll this buy me?" He dropped one of the silver planchets onto the plank. Even with the boisterous miners lined up on either side, the metallic ringing was music to the barkeep's ears.

"Pick your poison, mister. Any bottle you want, it's yours."

"The one closest to hand," Slocum decided.

"You're a man after my own heart." The barkeep set the bottle down and placed a dirty shot glass beside it. Slocum ignored the glass and drank from the bottle. He had poured just about every potion known to man down his gullet, but this choked him.

"That's got quite a kick to it."

"Learned my trade along the Mississippi, on riverboats," the barkeep said. "Burn a dozen peach pits and soak 'em in nitric acid overnight and you got a fine brandy when you add enough alcohol. I didn't have the peach pits, so I just tossed in the nitric acid with the pop skull."

"Best in town," said the miner to Slocum's left.

"None better in all of Arizona Territory," opined the miner on his right. Both men looked longingly at the bottle Slocum held. "That's the kind of booze that kin git you knee-walkin' drunk in a hurry."

Before he knew it, Slocum was pouring drinks for them, too, swilling the powerful brew between the miners' stories of increasingly improbable derring-do and riches lost and to be won.

An hour later Slocum wasn't feeling any pain. The aches and bruises he had accumulated from the mine disappeared into the distance and a warmth in his gut spread to fill his whole body. He had gotten to thinking about a different kind of warmth and building it with Autumn next to him in a feather bed, when he looked up to see the marshal aiming a shotgun at him.

"You make a move for that smoke wagon of yours and I'll splatter you all over the bar."

"Not much of a bar," Slocum said. His head spun from the booze as he tried to make sense of everything. "Why'd you want to shoot me, Marshal?"

"I got it on good authority you robbed the silver shipment to Benson. Gunned down two of my friends and stole six bags of silver."

"Six?" Slocum was drunk enough that he almost corrected the lawman by telling him he had only two.

"How'd he pay for his whiskey?"

"Don't remember, Marshal," the barkeep said. He made shooing motions behind the lawman's back, as if this would get rid of Slocum and the possibility of blood being spewed out of his lifeless corpse.

"You're a damn liar, Thomas."

"If'n he paid for his whiskey with one of them stolen coins, you'd want it for evidence, wouldn't you?"

"You know the law."

"Filthy, sweat-soaked scrip. That's how he paid for it."

"You lyin' son of a bitch," the marshal snarled. "I'll deal with you later, but now I got to get Slocum here to the jail. He's a real desperado."

"Like there ain't a dozen others even worse in Tombstone," muttered one of Slocum's drinking buddies. "An' they won't stand a thirsty miner fer so much as one drink. Not like him."

"And they don't listen to our stories, neither," said the other.

Slocum considered getting help from his two newfound friends, then knew they'd end up dead, too. The marshal's finger turned white on the double triggers. At this range he wouldn't miss, no matter how Slocum dodged. Worse, the marshal would be sure to take both miners and a couple of the other incautious, curious patrons with him.

Slocum considered the risk, and then a deputy snatched his Colt from his holster, eliminating any chance he might have of escaping.

"Git movin', Slocum. You know the way to the jail. You visited Autumn Dupree there often enough."

"You lock her up again, too?"

The whiskey fog burned off fast when he saw the expression on the marshal's face.

"You have her in jail?"

"Not a bit of it. She's the one who told us where to find you. Miz Dupree's a fine, upstandin' citizen of this town."

"Upstanding," grumbled a miner. "Damn shame such a fine woman ain't got a line of men standin' up, waitin' fer her to lay down fer 'em."

"'Nuff of that. Come along, Slocum, or there's gonna be a mess here to clean up." The marshal looked around and grumbled. "Maybe not so much anybody'd notice. Your blood'd drain straight into the ground 'fore anybody could grab that bottle of yours."

As he spoke, the marshal snatched the bottle away from Slocum and poked him with the shotgun. Slocum almost reacted, then knew the deputy behind him would likely shoot him down with his own six-shooter. He stepped out into the hot sun and let the two lawmen poke and prod him along to the jail.

He stopped just inside the door, his eyes adjusting to the dimness within. The marshal shoved him hard, forcing him to grab onto cell bars to keep from falling.

"Don't reckon you'd be happy sharin' a cell, so you each get one of your own."

While the deputy opened a second cell door, the marshal kept an eagle eye on Slocum. Only when the lock snapped shut did the marshal relax. He set the whiskey down on the desk and motioned for his deputy to get a pair of glasses from a cabinet to one side of the office.

Slocum watched carefully, seeing what was in the drawer other than the glasses. He said nothing when the deputy shoved the Colt in and closed it. Slocum knew where he had to go to retrieve his six-gun when he broke out of the jail.

"She put a noose around your neck, too, I see."

Slocum turned to the other prisoner and simply stared at Russ Atkins.

"You don't believe me? That's how I got here. She framed me. Bet she framed you, too. What for?"

"This owlhoot killed two friends of mine in a silver robbery," the marshal said, smacking his lips at the potent whiskey. The deputy made a face and reared back, as if he wanted to spit it out but knew better than to hawk a gob on the marshal's desk. The deputy put the empty glass on the edge of the desk, muttered something about making his rounds, and left.

One down, one to go. Slocum wasn't sure how he could dupe the marshal into getting close enough to give up the keys to the cell, but he would. At the moment, the marshal looked happy enough to sit across the room, swill the nitric acid–laced whiskey, and lord it over his prisoners.

"Did you, Slocum?"

"What'd you get locked up for, Atkins?"

"They claimed I killed Judge Alvarez."

"You shot the son of a bitch in the back. I never cottoned much to him, but he was a judge. Ain't gonna matter how much you bribed the other judges. Even that robber-in-robes Ernie Watkins won't stay bought when it comes to convictin' a judge-killer. Judge killing's a worse crime in their eyes than 'bout anything else."

"Fancy that," Slocum said. He watched how Russ Atkins reacted. If he had to bet on it, he would go with Atkins being innocent.

"You're saying Autumn killed the judge?"

"She was banging him. She had the opportunity to do about anything she wanted—including framing me."

"That's one way to keep you from filing a claim for the Silver Chalice Mine."

Atkins looked sharply at Slocum. Then he smiled ruefully.

"Why'd she frame you?"

"Loose ends," Slocum said. He had thought on the matter all the way from the saloon to the jail cell, and this was the best he could come up with. He had served her purpose and now she wanted the field clear of other players. Dead in the mine shaft, he was no good to her. Alive and kicking, he could be framed for just about anything. Why she had chosen to blame him for the silver robbery was something he couldn't figure out, except that it was an otherwise unsolved crime and the marshal would believe her without any proof.

"Makes sense," Atkins said.

"What about her other sister?"

"Summer?" Atkins shook his head. "All she wants is to be left alone. Might be she would even pin a medal on Autumn for killing that worthless husband of hers."

"Jerome Lorritsen?"

"He was a layabout and Summer tried to keep him working their claim, but Spring lured him away."

"With silver?" Slocum knew the sisters looked enough alike to be triplets, so leaving one for another wasn't trading up to a better-looking woman. But Summer might have refused to perform her wifely duties until he worked harder, and Spring would never do that. If anything, Spring would have kept Jerome from his work.

"Autumn is a real bitch. She twists men around her little finger and then flicks them away," Atkins said glumly. "I hope you got something out of this, Slocum."

"All either of you's gonna get is a rope necktie," the marshal said. He poured himself another shot of the potent whiskey. Slocum saw that the marshal's hand wobbled just a little. He didn't appreciate how powerful the whiskey was. Slocum didn't know how it would benefit him if the marshal passed out at the desk, since the keys were hanging at the marshal's belt.

"I hate to say it, but he's right," Atkins said. "A dead judge, dead shipping guards and drivers, we're up shit creek."

"If you think I did rob the silver shipment, Marshal," Slocum said, "what would it be worth recovering the silver?"

"You confessin', Slocum? Didn't expect that of you. You have the look of a man who'd go to the gallows with your tater trap closed—even as the trapdoor under you was sprung."

"Clarke and Gunnison are the road agents you want," Slocum said. "You catch them, you have the killers." He paused as the marshal eyed him sharply. "And you can get all the silver from them."

"There was three robbers? That what you're sayin'? They was your partners?"

"How do you know there were three? I only know of two," Slocum said. "Clarke and Gunnison."

The marshal's gimlet gaze fogged over as the effects of the alcohol washed back across his brain.

"Might look 'em up, yeah," the marshal said. His words slurred now, and when he poured himself another shot, he missed and spilled some of the liquid on the desk. The fizzing drops chewed away the varnish.

Slocum and Atkins exchanged knowing looks. The same thought ran through both men's minds. This might be the only chance they got to get the hell out of Tombstone. How that would happen was still a mystery. Unless the marshal came closer, they'd never be able to reach the key ring dangling at his belt.

"So, Marshal, you're not going to share your bounty with us? You've got us dead to rights," said Atkins. "Why not let us have a snort of that fine whiskey?"

Slocum saw what the man was trying, but the marshal waved Atkins off. If anything, drinking in front of his prisoners suited the lawman better than sharing. He could torment them with the sight of whiskey being consumed. No shred of human decency remained in the man's breast.

But Slocum saw another course of action.

"He's right, Marshal. Share it. I paid for it, after all."

"With one of them silver slugs they was shippin'," the marshal said. He almost fell out of his desk chair. "I shoulda taken it from the barkeep as evidence, of course."

"Of course," Slocum said. "You were too busy doing your duty, locking me up. You should celebrate catching such a desperado."

"Damn right, Slocum." The marshal knocked back another shot. He belched and reached for the bottle but couldn't find it.

Atkins started to say something, but Slocum motioned

him to silence. Slocum watched the marshal closely. The man crossed his arms on the desk and laid his head on them. He started snoring immediately.

"Fire!" Slocum yelled at the top of his lungs. "The jail's on fire!"

Atkins was a second slow understanding what Slocum was up to. Then he joined in with his own dire warnings of everyone dying in the fire.

The marshal jerked upright, fell from the chair, and called out, "Fire?"

"Fire!"

"Damn, what happened?"

"Get out, Marshal. Save yourself before the flames kill you. I'm in the street," Slocum shouted. "Come to my voice."

The lawman took a wobbly step, turned, and lurched in the direction of the jail cells. Slocum grabbed him around the neck and jerked the man's head hard into the iron bars. The marshal went limp and sank down. Slocum made a grab and caught the key ring before it got out of reach.

It took only a second to open his cell.

"Slocum, you can't leave me," Atkins said. "I helped you lure him over. We're both Autumn's dupes."

Slocum threw the keys to Atkins, who caught them and worked open his own cell door. Slocum turned his back on Atkins as he opened the drawer with his Colt Navy in it.

"Slow Joe," Slocum heard before something hard crashed into the top of his head, knocking him to the floor.

13

"Move along. Keep walking or I'll kill you here and let you fry in the sun."

"Gotta keep walkin'," Slocum said, his head feeling as if it would explode. "Wanna get away."

"That's right. Get away from the law."

"Wha—" Slocum felt another sharp blow on the side of his head that drove him to his knees.

"Come on," came the insistent command.

Slocum couldn't focus to understand what was happening. He remembered getting free of the jail cell, but the echoes of a name refused to come back to him. He had been hit on the head after he heard a name. A name.

Slow Joe!

He fought to get away, but the hand holding his arm was too strong. Another blow drove him to his knees. The hand dragged him awhile in the dirt, rocks cutting at his legs until he got his feet under him again.

"Get on your horse."

Slocum squinted hard and saw Russ Atkins beside him, pistol in his hand. When Atkins saw that Slocum was recovering from being hit, he reared back, swung, and landed his pistol barrel on Slocum's head. Slocum blacked out.

When Slocum awoke, he found it hard to breathe. He slowly understood that he was slung belly-down over the saddle and had been lashed into place. As the desert bounced by in his field of vision, he tensed and relaxed to test the limits of his bonds. He was hogtied too securely to get free. Not sure how long he had ridden, he tried to crane his neck around and get a gander at the sun to estimate the time of day. It was cooler—a little. The sun might be hanging low in the distance, but Slocum couldn't see to the west. He caught sight of the Dragoon Mountains and a part of Goose Flats he thought he recognized.

North. They rode north. He wasn't sure what good knowing this did, but it let him relax a mite. Any information he could gather gave him a better chance to figure out what was going on. Escaping from the Tombstone jail had been easy enough, but he had never expected Russ Atkins to slug him.

If the man had a bone to pick, leaving Slocum in the jail would have settled matters once and for all. When the marshal came to, he would have been likely to lynch any prisoner who had taken part in the escape. The lawman didn't strike Slocum as a forgiving soul.

So why had Atkins slugged him?

"Slow Joe," Slocum grated out. He remembered hearing that before Atkins hit him. The name of the robber he had robbed—and the one Gunnison and Clarke had killed—had leaked from Atkins's lips for a reason. They weren't related, Slocum didn't think, since the men looked nothing alike. That didn't mean too much, but Slocum would have noticed even a slight family resemblance the first time he had seen Atkins. He had been keyed up and alert for anything that might give away his own theft of the silver.

It took some bouncing along, but Slocum finally came to the conclusion that Atkins had been the brains behind the robbery. Clarke and Gunnison couldn't find a whorehouse in Tombstone without a map. Slow Joe had been aptly named. Atkins must have found out about the silver shipment, planned the robbery, and then waited for his partners to rob the wagon. Killing the silver wagon's team had been a mistake. Atkins might have wanted them to drive away. With the horses dead, the trio had each taken a part of the silver shipment, intending to get together later in Tombstone. From there, they could fetch the stashes of silver and divvy it up. But Slocum had stolen Slow Joe's share and Clarke and Gunnison had killed their partner.

This made Slocum change his reasoning about why Gunnison had tried to steal the Silver Chalice. Atkins had ordered them to do so to make Autumn give up her attempt to claim the deed as her own. Slocum had thought Atkins had gone to the mine, but he hadn't—he had ridden somewhere else, and Slocum had run afoul of his partners.

"Whoa!"

Slocum's horse obeyed, and he rocked back and forth. For a moment, he thought he would slide off, but ropes around his ankles kept him slung over the saddle. A shadow moved on the ground until Slocum stared at Atkins's boots.

"You're awake. Don't try fooling me none," Atkins said. The whisper of steel across leather sounded an instant before Slocum crashed to the ground. Atkins had cut the ropes holding him onto the horse but not the bonds on his wrists behind his back.

Slocum couldn't contain the moan as he rolled over and fought to sit up. His feet were free, but with his hands tied the way they were, he couldn't get to his feet. He looked up to see the setting sun glint off the knife in Atkins's hand.

"I ought to slit your throat."

"I got you out of jail. Why'd you want to go and kill me? Didn't Autumn set up both up? We have that in common."

"You killed Slow Joe and robbed him."

"Clarke and Gunnison killed him. Are they your partners?"

"You've got it all figured out. Of course they're my partners."

"You planned the robbery, but you weren't there. Why not?"

"I had to stay in Tombstone because the mine superintendent had caught a whiff of my plans, and I had to deal with him before he could telegraph ahead. I didn't want my gang getting caught by the sheriff over in Benson."

"Who spilled your plot?"

Atkins hesitated, then said, "Could have been any of those dimwits. It didn't matter because everything went fine."

"They killed the driver and guard. Why not strand them and steal the wagon with the silver in it?"

"I didn't say the plan went exactly right. They shot the horses by accident. You shut up, Slocum. You shut up except for telling me what you did with the silver Slow Joe got."

"They tried to cut you out, didn't they? They split the silver three ways, not four."

"I want Slow Joe's share," Atkins said, "and I'm not too fussy about getting it. Tell me and you can die real quick. Make me squeeze it out of you and, well, I know tricks the Apaches use on their prisoners. I've come across the carcasses of men who lasted for, oh, two days, maybe three."

Slocum wasn't all that scared of Atkins's threats. He tried to figure out how he could drive a wedge between him and his partners.

"They may see their way clear to killing you so you're not breathing down their necks all the time," Slocum said. "You told them to dynamite the Silver Chalice, but maybe they have designs on the mine themselves. Why not? Let Autumn have her way with you. That'd have you rolling in clover, wouldn't it?"

"They do what I tell them," Atkins said. "Between them, they don't have the sense God gave a goose."

"Don't need to have good sense to cross you. They killed Slow Joe and took his share. If you think they're going to split the take with you . . ." Slocum let his words trail off so Atkins could work on them awhile himself. Everything Slocum said was true—except for Clarke and Gunnison having Slow Joe's share of the silver. If he so much as hinted that he had it, he was a dead man.

"I ought to shoot you here and now."

"You won't," Slocum said, keeping his words slow and regular, no matter that he wanted to blurt them out. "If you think I know where the missing silver is, killing me will make for certain sure you never find it. But I don't have it. Clarke and Gunnison do."

"Then there's no reason not to kill you."

"But you don't believe me," Slocum went on. "You think I killed Slow Joe and took his silver."

"You did it. I feel it in my bones."

"Because Clarke and Gunnison are too stupid to ever steal anything or kill anybody," Slocum said, seeing his jibe hit Atkins hard. There wasn't any trust between the men. Slocum's half truths worked to widen the chasm between them.

"I'll find out what you know. I swear to God I will!"

The blow caught Slocum on the cheek and knocked him flat. He went down heavily, rolled, and tried to get to his feet, but Atkins launched a kick that ended in Slocum's arched belly. The air left him in a giant rush, and he was paralyzed as Atkins staked him out.

By the time his lungs worked again and some sense had returned, Slocum found himself in a dire situation. He lay flat on his back staring up at the twilight sky. His wrists and ankles were secured to stakes driven into the hard ground. Strain as he might, he couldn't budge the stakes.

"Rawhide strips," Atkins told him. "I used rawhide to bind you. Wet rawhide. As the cord dries, it will shrink and pull you apart. Oh, it won't yank your arms and legs off, but it'll be even more uncomfortable than it is now. When the sun comes up, the drying will go even faster. I reckon you'll be feelin' real pain by then."

"And I'll be staring at the sun all day till I go blind."

"I could cut off your eyelids like the Apaches do," Atkins said, "but I want to leave something in reserve. You're a hard one, Slocum, and I need to offer you a tad more torture if you don't sing out where you hid the silver."

"Don't have it. Clarke does. Him and Gunnison. Your partners."

"Not what I wanted to hear." Atkins poured water on the rawhide strips and then towered over Slocum, making sure Slocum could see him drink a long draft from the canteen. When he finished, he upended the canteen and let a few remaining drops trickle across Slocum's face.

"That's all the water you're going to get unless you talk."

"Moon's coming up," Slocum said. "Real purty right about now. Be full soon."

"It'll be a blood moon," Atkins said coldly. "Your blood."

He stalked off. Slocum craned his neck up to see that Atkins worked to build a campfire a half dozen yards away. Before long the odor of cooking oatmeal mixed with the mesquite wood smoke. Slocum had lived on oatmeal and damned little else for long spells, especially when he was making his way across the prairie, and he didn't have much of a yen for it. But now his belly would wrap itself around about anything edible. If he could have reached them, he would have eaten the rawhide strips on his wrists.

It might have been imagination, but he felt as if the drying rawhide already pulled him a bit more spread-eagle on the desert floor. Ants nipped at his flesh, but compared to the cactus spines in his butt, that was nothing. Atkins hadn't picked the worst spot to stake him out, but he hadn't been too charitable about clearing off a stretch of desert, either.

Slocum watched the moon rise and then sink in the distance. Twisting and turning got him nowhere. The stakes

Atkins had driven into the ground were too firmly buried to budge. Lacking any leverage, Slocum wasn't sure he could have pulled himself free even if they had been sunk down only a few inches.

"You want to tell me where the silver is before I go to sleep, Slocum?"

"Go to hell."

"You'll be there 'fore me, I guarantee it. We can talk some more after the sun comes up. That might convince you how serious I am."

Slocum tried to relax but couldn't. He closed his eyes, but sleep never came. The ants and the cactus spines and his aching joints prevented any rest. His thoughts spun out of control as he tried to come up with ways to get free from Atkins. Killing the outlaw would be high on the list. Slocum would do it using his bare hands, but already his fingers felt like bloated sausages. The strips cut off circulation and made handling even a six-shooter out of the question.

If he told Atkins where the silver was hidden, he would buy himself a day or two, but once the outlaw assured himself he had Slow Joe's portion, he would kill Slocum. There wasn't anything Slocum could offer more than the silver to stay alive.

Teaming up to get even with Autumn crossed his mind, but Atkins was able to do that without Slocum. And he probably would, especially if he got the silver from the robbery. With that much money he could buy judges left and right and maybe even the marshal. The lawman had taken a bit too eagerly to the bottle not to have weak spots to exploit.

The eastern horizon brightened with false dawn. Slocum knew his hours were numbered now. It would get darker and then the sun would pop above the horizon and his real torment would begin. He didn't know how long he would last before he told Atkins where the silver was just to be put out of his misery. As much as dying without telling the outlaw appealed to him, Slocum wasn't sure he could last that

long. Although during the war he had endured wounds that
would have killed another man.

When he had protested the Lawrence, Kansas, raid, Quantrill had Bloody Bill Anderson shoot Slocum in the gut and
leave him to die. Spite and sheer force of will had kept
Slocum moving, refusing to die. He had found shelter and
spent days weaker than a kitten before he had fought his
way back to a semblance of strength. Even then he hadn't
been up to fighting strength for months and months, most
of that spent at the family farm in Georgia gathering energy
and finding a different reason each day to live.

He wished he could have evened the score with Bill
Anderson and William Quantrill, but fate had partly done
that for him. He'd heard Quantrill's skull had ended up in a
sideshow somewhere in his home state of Ohio. Slocum
would have paid good money to see the skull, just to shatter
it with six shots from his pistol.

The false dawn began to dim and so did his hopes.

He lay back staring up at the stars. This would be the
last time he ever saw them. The sun would boil into the
desert sky and blind him before noon. Turning his head to
one side to examine the strips on his wrist one more time
caused him to stiffen and raise up as far as he could.

Movement. Shadows. Coyotes might dine on him before
he died from the sun. But the shadow moved, and he knew
no four-legged animal walked like that. New fear raced
through him. Apaches roamed the entire territory, trying to
get their land back from the white eyes. He might have
been unfortunate enough to be discovered by a band of
Chiricahua. If they found a white man staked out, they
would never free him. The best he could hope for would be
Atkins staked out alongside him, sharing his torture.

More movement. Darting away. He shifted and looked
toward Atkins's camp. He could warn the man, but why
bother? There wasn't any gain in it for Slocum. The one

time he had rescued Atkins—from the Tombstone jail—he had ended up staked out on the desert.

He held his tongue. Even if he had wanted, Slocum wasn't sure he could have done more than a gurgle deep in his throat. His tongue felt like his fingers, all bloated and tingly. He looked around for more sign that they weren't alone in the desert, but he saw nothing.

Then he heard the soft crunch of footsteps near his head. He arched his neck but couldn't see. A hand clamped down over his mouth.

"Don't talk. I'll get you free in a minute."

He knew the voice—and yet he didn't. If the hand hadn't remained over his mouth, he might have cried out in pain when a knife severed the bonds on his right hand and circulation tried to return to his hand.

A woman hunched down at his left side, sawing with her knife to cut through the rawhide. He was ready for the pain when the strip finally parted.

"I'll get your feet next. Just lie there. Don't rouse him."

Slocum twitched but was otherwise unable to move. The ant bites and spines in his body burned with renewed ferocity now that his hands were no longer the main source of pain. He slid his arms down to his sides and clumsily lifted them onto his belly so he could rub them together. Needles of returning circulation danced, but even if he could take the knife from the woman, he would not have been able to use it on Atkins.

"Can you stand?"

Through pure force of will, Slocum sat up and massaged his legs. For the first time he got a look at the woman.

He caught his breath. He thought the shadow-cloaked face was that of Autumn Dupree. Then he realized the other sister had rescued him.

"Summer?"

"Shhh. He'll hear you. Can you hold this?" She forced

his Colt Navy into his hands. Slocum dropped it, then fumbled and retrieved it. Then she took it from him and rammed it into his cross-draw holster. "We have to get out of here before he wakes up. You're in no condition to fight him."

"I'll shoot the bastard in his sleep." He paused, then asked, "Why didn't you do that? He's alone."

"I . . . I never killed anyone. I couldn't do it."

"Even to save my life? Your own life?"

"Please, there's no time. It'll be light soon."

Slocum knew she was right. With Summer's aid he got to his feet and shuffled away. Every step brought more strength to his body, but he still trembled. Holding his six-shooter would be out of the question. Deep gashes around his wrists oozed blood now, turning his palms and fingers slippery.

"I have your horse."

"Get Atkins's, too. Strand the bastard out here on foot."

"I cut the cinch on his saddle. That was the best I could do. His horse was too skittish to get near. Yours was a lot friendlier."

Slocum let Summer Lorritsen help him into the saddle. He had ridden to this spot belly down. Now he was riding off like a man. But he wished he could deal with Russ Atkins.

She grabbed the reins since he couldn't hang on to them and led him away, back in the direction of Tombstone.

He couldn't even the score with Atkins now. But he would. He definitely would.

14

"We can't go back to Tombstone," Slocum said. "The marshal is going to be hunting for my scalp and might not want to let me stand trial."

"I heard," Summer Lorritsen said. "It made quite a splash the way you got him drunk and then scared him to death like you did."

"He's dead?"

"Oh, that's just a figure of speech," Summer said. "He's alive and furious since he's the laughingstock of town. That will make him even more dangerous for you. I intend to go to my mine. You can hole up there for a spell."

"Until?"

Summer looked at him. He felt as if both of her sisters were wrapped up into this single woman. Her blue eyes bored into him and made him feel as if he wasn't anything more than a bug under a magnifying glass—and yet there was something more he couldn't quite put his finger on.

"You tried to find who killed my husband," she said unexpectedly.

"That's why I rode up to your claim the first time."

I don't blame you for not telling me Jerome was dead then. I found out from a drifter leaving Tombstone, heading for Mesilla, but I think I'd figured out what was going on after you left. Jerome was a lazy no-account, but thank you for trying. Did you ever figure out who did it?"

"Never did," Slocum said, "but Atkins might be a candidate for that job," he said. "He and three others robbed a silver shipment. Two of the three killed the third one of the gang to steal his share, but the other two are working hand-in-glove with Atkins."

"You think they might have done it? Or just Spring's husband?"

Slocum shrugged. The bodies were piling up, and he didn't know who might be next. While he doubted it, Spring might have had something to do with Jerome's death. She had a willing worker but might have thought she could replace him with Slocum, after their night together. When she could have done it herself was a matter he could never resolve—there simply was no way she had left the bed and killed her willing miner. That didn't rule out her hiring someone to do it, but Slocum didn't see any sense in that. Spring could have killed Jerome in any of a dozen ways, and nobody would have been the wiser. Someone had ridden up, plugged him, and then hightailed it.

"Will you keep looking?"

"Don't see the payoff," Slocum admitted. "I've got a price on my head now. As you said, the marshal didn't cotton much to being made to look foolish."

"Is it possible Autumn did it?"

Slocum sat a little straighter in the saddle. He hadn't really considered the other sister, but it might have happened that way, especially since he had found out how treacherous the woman could be.

"You have proof?"

"None, but she's one sneaky bitch."

Slocum looked hard at Summer. He hadn't heard the

woman speak with such venom before, and this was her own sister.

"I'm not arguing that," he said.

Summer laughed, but there was no humor in it.

"Papa would never have left either of them the Silver Chalice. He would have wanted me to have it, free and clear."

"You and Jerome? How'd your pa get along with your husband?"

"Papa was a good judge of character, though I never realized how good until after he died. He and Jerome never got along. I couldn't figure out why because I was in love with him then, but Papa saw his bad points."

"What about Spring and Autumn's husbands?"

"Russ Atkins was never around much. I don't think he ever cared for Spring and might have had it in mind to inherit the Silver Chalice, but Autumn's husband lit out before Papa ever met him."

"You sure Andre Dupree returned to France?"

"He made a good case for going to New Orleans and sailing from there. He might have been the only one—other than me—who saw Autumn for what she was. He wised up and left."

"Autumn might have killed the judge. That's what Atkins said, and I'm inclined to believe him now. He had nothing to gain from killing anyone hearing the case, not when he had his own judge bribed."

"Watkins," Summer said. Her lips thinned to a line as she stared at the desert ahead. The sun had heated the ground enough to cause the horizon to turn into shimmery silver. Slocum wondered what she saw in the distant mirage, and it probably wasn't the elusive promise of water that was never there.

"You know the politics better than I do. Does Autumn have a chance to be named sole owner of the mine?"

"Yeah."

"But you want the Silver Chalice for yourself?"

"I deserve it!"

"Without some pull in court, you don't have much chance. Between Atkins and your sister, they have the crooked judges covered."

"Russ doesn't matter now. Nobody's going to believe he didn't kill Judge Alvarez. It's Autumn we have to worry about."

Slocum didn't answer because he didn't like being included in Summer's "we." She had some scheme in mind, and he wasn't inclined to help her. She looked at him when he said nothing. Her blue eyes were like daggers stabbing into his green ones.

"I saved you. I know I ought to have killed Russ, but that doesn't matter. I kept you from dying what would have been a painful death."

"Thanks," Slocum said.

"There's my claim. Let's get in out of the sun. I could use a drink."

"Water?"

Summer laughed.

"I don't know what my sisters drink—drank—but I need something more powerful to keep me working the claim. Since Jerome left, I've done all the work myself. All of it." A touch of bitterness gilded her words.

Slocum put their horses under a tarp strung off the side of the cabin. It afforded a little shade, but more than this, two wood buckets furnished water. The horses could drink and not bloat. He unsaddled them and rubbed them down, made sure they had newly filled buckets, and only then went to the cabin door.

It was dim inside and cooler. The cabin had been built against the side of a hill to afford some protection from the brutal sun. Summer sat at a table with a half-full bottle of whiskey and two glasses on it.

"Take a load off. There's plenty for both of us." She gestured toward the whiskey and then the chair opposite her.

Slocum sank into the chair. He groaned when his joints all protested at the same instant.

"I need this more'n I thought," he said. His hands were a mite clumsy yet. Summer poured for them both. She held up the shot glass and waited for him to lift his in silent toast. They both knocked back the liquor. Slocum expected a mule's kick that never came.

"That's mighty smooth," he said.

"They lace a lot of whiskey in town with poisons you couldn't believe."

"Nitric acid," he said. Her eyebrows arched.

"I hadn't heard that. Some put in arsenic. Others boil loco weed and pour the liquid into their trade whiskey. You drink that and you can claw your own stomach out." She poured another. Slocum downed it but didn't feel any of it leaking into his guts through holes already burned there from his earlier drinking in Tombstone. His pain faded away, even if enough lingered to remind him of what Russ Atkins had done to him.

He owed Clarke and Gunnison. He added Atkins to the list of men to get even with.

"Take your revenge on him by helping me get clear title to the Silver Chalice," Summer said unexpectedly.

"You've got a one-track mind."

"I'm sick of killing myself in this worthless hole-in-the-ground. Papa should have split the mine among all of his children."

"Would you be willing to split the ownership?" Slocum saw a curious play of emotion on the woman's lovely face.

She nodded slowly. "I likely would, but I think I can convince a court to give it to me."

"What proof do you have?" Slocum tensed when Summer stood and began unfastening her bodice. She flashed him a wicked smile and continued unfastening the front until she also flashed him a nice pair of breasts. She pulled a rolled-up sheet of paper from this luscious hiding place.

"The forged will. Spring had it and I took it."

"When?"

"Does it matter, John? I can show that the will is a fraud. That throws the ownership up for any of the children. Autumn killed her pet judge. It might be that Judge Watkins is still bought and paid for by Russ, but his position is a lot weaker now. The judge is nobody's fool and might not even hear the case."

"Who would?"

"A judge brought in from Bisbee or Fairbank. It won't matter as long as he's not scared of Autumn or Russ."

She pushed the bogus will across the table toward Slocum. She had to lean forward slightly to do so. Her blouse fell open all the way, giving him an unrestricted view of her twin peaks. The tips were hard and visibly pulsing. She breathed a little faster and made no move to cover her nakedness.

Slocum reached out, almost in spite of himself, to touch one of the dangling teats. She didn't move away. Summer closed her eyes and let out a soft sigh.

"That feels good, John. So good."

"Do you want more?" His hand already slipped down the valley between her breasts and across her belly. She gasped when he moved even lower, working his hand under the waistband of her skirt. His fingers brushed across a fleecy patch but could move no farther because of the angle. He stood slowly, and she moved around the table, pressing close.

His hand slid lower and his finger curled about, entering her. He had to support her with his left arm to keep her from swooning.

"You've made me weak in the knees since I first laid eyes on you," she said in a sex-husky voice. "Now lay me. I want you, John. I do!"

He cut off her words with a deep kiss. His lips were chapped, but the whiskey had taken the edge off any pain. Their tongues began dancing about, teasing and tormenting each other until their mutual passion passed the point of no return.

Slocum spun her about and sat her on the table. The whiskey crashed to the dirt floor. Neither noticed. Summer lifted her feet and braced them on the edge of the table so her knees were raised. He moved his hands down to her ankles and slowly worked his way up both legs simultaneously. Her skirt lifted and exposed her fully.

Dropping to his knees, Slocum fumbled around and found the whiskey bottle. Some remained. He poured a few drops onto her privates. Summer caught her breath.

"That's so cold!"

Slocum lapped at it. For an instant he was deaf and blind as her thighs clamped firmly on either side of his head. Then she relaxed and allowed him to pull back. He poured more of the whiskey across her nether lips and sucked it up. The woman's body quivered now with every touch of his tongue. He invaded her once more with a finger as he kept up the oral assault. Summer dropped back onto the table, propped on her elbows.

She moaned constantly now. The incoherent sounds told Slocum she wanted more of what he had to offer. He stood, looking down at her so wantonly open to him. Her breasts quivered as the nub perched atop each turned into a hard, pink cap. He dripped some whiskey on each, let it evaporate a moment to give her a thrill of cold, then applied his hot lips. When she was gasping and crying out, he knocked back the last of the whiskey and kissed her full on the lips.

The liquor set them both ablaze. She clawed at his shirt, peeling it away. Then they both worked to get his gunbelt off and his jeans down. It was Slocum's turn to gasp when she freed his manhood, now standing tall and proud. Her fingers gripped him and insistently tugged him to the spot where he had dripped the whiskey only minutes before.

He moved forward as Summer scooted over on the table. Slocum slid his hands up under her armpits so he could hold her shoulders. She held on to the edge of the table. This gave them all the leverage they needed. Slocum had intended to move slowly, working up a head of steam. But she was so tight and hot and moist around him, he had to possess her immediately. His hips flew like a shuttlecock. He drove forward, sank balls deep, and then pulled back just as fast.

Friction mounted and burned at him. Deep down in his loins a tiny spark caught fire and turned into a raging conflagration that devoured him entirely. The hot tide rose within him and then exploded as he plunged back into her needy interior. Summer clung fiercely to him. Her hips rose to meet him, and they ground their crotches together as Slocum spent himself. It seemed to last forever and yet was over all too quickly.

He looked down at her flushed face. The glow extended all the way down to the tops of her breasts.

"You're dripping sweat on me," she said. She reached up and gently pushed his lank black hair from his eyes. "It's all matted with sweat."

"You brought it out of me," he said.

Summer laughed. Slocum thought of bells ringing. And then she dropped her legs on either side of his hips and pulled herself up to drop to the floor. She clung to him a moment, her face pressed into his chest.

"You're sweaty all over."

"You didn't complain a couple minutes ago."

"No, no, I didn't," she said in a voice almost too low for him to hear. Louder she said, "Let's take a bath. I saved up some water."

"If it's outside, it's likely boiling hot."

"Like you felt inside me," Summer said.

Slocum kissed her and she rubbed against him, her tits crushing against his chest. Then she pushed him away.

"We shouldn't do this."

"I didn't hear you complain," he repeated.

"It's not that, John. It's just—it's just I don't dare fall for you. They'll use that against me. Every time I ever loved anyone or anything, it got used against me."

"Your sisters?"

Summer nodded. "They're evil bitches. Both of them. Then there's—" She saw his reaction and quickly said, "I need your help, John. I do. I can't fight her alone. I'll present the evidence of the fake will and throw everything into a cocked hat. All I need is your support."

"This is crazy," Slocum said. "You might win, but would you want to be partners with Autumn, if that's the way the judge decides?"

"I'd be partners with them. Let them buy me out. Then I—we—could go off together. There are better places than this."

Slocum couldn't help but notice the way Summer still referred to her sisters as "them," in spite of Spring being dead. Summer had quite a family.

"Just sell this mine for what you can and leave. Go back East. This desert is no place for a pretty woman like you."

"You think I'm pretty?" Summer tried to push her disheveled hair into some semblance of order. Slocum had to laugh. She was still half-naked and preening, as if this would bring him around to agreeing to help her.

"Quit fishing for compliments. You know you are." Slocum didn't add that physically the three sisters were like peas in a pod. He knew the differences between them, but only from making love to each of them. If they all got gussied up—the ones that were still alive—it might be hard to put names to them. They weren't triplets, but their heritage was obvious.

"Help me, John. Please."

Slocum cursed himself, but he found himself nodding. He need only retrieve the silver he had buried south of town and he could go live in Mexico in style, with a bottle of tequila in one hand and a pretty señorita in the other. But right now he had Summer Lorritsen.

He damned himself for a fool, but he owed her. No matter what, John Slocum always paid his debts. She had risked her life to rescue him from Russ Atkins. He owed her, but when the ownership of the Silver Chalice Mine was decided, whichever way it went, he was riding away from Tombstone. Fast.

She kissed him again, and he forgot about his future and exchanged it for the here and now.

15

"There's no reason for me to risk going into town," Slocum said. He knew he could more than stand up to the marshal, but getting a posse or, worse, a lynch mob, on his trail made him a touch uneasy. It was broad daylight so he could be recognized, and by now everyone in Tombstone had to know he had escaped from jail and humiliated the marshal doing so. All that was necessary for the word to get around was to let Maude find out.

"I need your support, John," Summer said earnestly. She reached over and took his arm. Her fingers were hot and sweaty, but he couldn't complain. After riding most of the day in the sun, he was sweaty, too, and the sleeves of his shirt and coat were matted to his arm. "Keep them from kidnapping me and all will be fine. I can get the deed to the mine. If not entirely in my name, then so we can split it three ways."

Slocum had started to point out that Atkins was not likely to be in the legal fray, when he spotted the marshal and a deputy rounding the corner at Fifth Street heading down Toughnut for the courthouse.

"I gotta hide," he said. Autumn tried to give him a quick

145

kiss, but Slocum wheeled his horse about and trotted toward Allen Street. It was early afternoon and the serious drinking hadn't started in the saloons yet, but that didn't keep the street from being crowded with miners come to town for supplies and the businessmen angling to sell them the over-priced goods.

He kept his hat pulled down and his bandanna up. From the way the dust fell off him, anyone glancing in his direction knew he had just come in off the trail. Looking neither left nor right, he rode down the street and circled back toward the courthouse, taking Fifth Street so he would come up from behind the marshal and his deputy, thinking they wouldn't bother checking behind themselves in town.

The plan worked. The two lawmen stood at the top of the steps, looking into the bowels of the building. Slocum dismounted and tethered his horse where he could get to it fast, if the need arose, then went around to the side of the courthouse. Windows stood open to catch even the slightest breeze blowing across the desert.

A faint gust of air from inside told him someone had a fan working. Slocum stood on tiptoe and peered inside. Two boys took turns at a crank spinning a wheel mounted with blades. The fan, probably taken from one of the mine ventilation systems, circulated the air in the stuffy courtroom, sending the hot air out and sucking in whatever cooler air there might be from the lobby.

Slocum found himself a crate, upended it, and more comfortably studied the room. The judge talked with two men in fancy coats. Slocum pegged them as lawyers. Autumn sat on the far side of the room, and Summer was only a few rows away from where Slocum peered in. He caught his breath when he saw Clarke at the rear of the large room. Gunnison was nowhere to be seen. Not a half dozen chairs away from Summer sat Winthrop. Slocum had no idea what his interest might be, but this was the kind of legal brawl that drew everyone in town like flies to cow flop.

He almost expected Russ Atkins to be present, maybe wearing a disguise, but if the man had chosen to attend, he was better camouflaged than Slocum could detect.

"Aw, right, time to get this sideshow started," the judge bellowed. The bailiff took over the task of calling the court to order and made everyone stand as the judge took the bench.

"The Right Honorable Judge Ernest Watkins, presiding," the bailiff said. "The matter before the court is the ownership of the Silver Chalice Mine."

"We know that, you damn fool," growled Watkins. "Let's get on with it."

The bailiff glared but motioned for the attorneys to approach the bench. Slocum noticed that while the lawyers talked privately the bailiff went to the rear of the courtroom and whispered to Clarke. The judge started hearing the arguments from Autumn's lawyer, but Slocum dropped to the ground and went to the courthouse steps in time to see Clarke hurrying down Toughnut Street.

Being careful to avoid any chance sighting by the marshal, Slocum mounted his horse and set off after Clarke. By the time he reached the edge of town, all he saw was a cloud of dust ahead of him on the road. Clarke rode like a demon through the hot afternoon sun. From the direction he took, Slocum figured he rode for the Silver Chalice. Whatever the bailiff said had lit his tail feathers and sent him fluttering in the direction of the mine.

Slocum took his sweet time since he knew where Clarke rode. There was no point killing his horse in the burning heat. He even rested his horse on occasion to be sure the mare was ready for whatever demands he put on her when he cornered Clarke.

It was somewhere past sundown when Slocum approached the mine. He heard someone swearing a blue streak. That had to be Clarke as he noisily hunted for whatever the bailiff had sent him after. Since the bailiff and Russ Atkins had been involved in some illicit business, Slocum guessed that the bailiff was double-crossing Atkins, now that the man was wanted for murder and jailbreak.

Slocum dismounted and advanced slowly, keeping to the shadows. Clarke stood some distance from the dross pile, prowling about, kicking at rocks seemingly at random. The outlaw stopped, threw his hands up in obvious frustration, then returned to his hunt, going downhill in his search for whatever eluded him. Slocum moved toward the cabin to get out of sight. In the gathering darkness, he doubted this would be much of a problem, but he didn't want to take chances. Too many things had gone against him since he had blundered onto the silver robbery along the Benson road.

Clarke continued his hunt. Slocum considered getting the drop on him, maybe even cutting him down without so much as a fare-thee-well, but his curiosity got the better of him. What had the bailiff said and what was Clarke hunting?

As he watched, Slocum got an uneasy feeling of someone else nearby. He stepped closer to the cabin and faded into complete shadows. He looked toward the mine and the hill above the mine's mouth. The sudden lance of orange flame from the muzzle of a rifle momentarily dazzled him. A second and third shot rang out.

Clarke cursed as he dived for cover, and the sniper cursed, too.

"You thought you'd left me fer dead," Gunnison called. "You son of a bitch. You can't leave me in the desert like that. I'd have died if an Apache hadn't come by and took pity on me. A goddamn Indian saved me! It was a shame to have to kill him, but I did. And I'm gonna kill you, too, you backstabbing bastard!"

Gunnison fired a few more times, but he only sent lead flying in an attempt to flush Clarke. Slocum couldn't see the object of Gunnison's wrath, and he doubted the sniper could, either.

Letting the men kill themselves was the smartest thing to do, but Slocum was powerful anxious to find what had brought Clarke to the mine—to the spot a dozen yards from the mine and away from the spent ore. Nothing of value ought to be where he hunted, yet he hadn't moved more than a few yards since Slocum had crept up.

Moving like a shadow himself, Slocum hiked a quarter mile into a spot where the hill holding the Silver Chalice sloped gradually upward. He climbed, got his bearings, and then came around to a spot he thought would be above Gunnison.

The sharp reports from the outlaw's rifle warned him when he neared. Slocum flopped on his belly and poked his head over a rocky ledge. Not ten feet below, Gunnison squatted, his rifle roving back and forth as he hunted for his target. Slocum looked downslope but couldn't pick out Clarke among the piles of rock. He was considering what he could do, when Clarke opened fire from below. This brought immediate return fire from Gunnison. Slocum kept his head down as lead ricocheted all around.

"It doesn't have to be this way, Gunnison. It's all a misunderstanding. Wasn't me what left you out there to die. It was Atkins. You know how he is. He'd slit his own grandmother's throat if there was a nickel in it."

"You killed him. I know you did. You're after his share of the loot."

"We can split it. Fifty-fifty."

"What about your new buddy, that fella workin' for the judge?"

"It was him that told me where Atkins hid the map. He scratched it on an envelope and hid it here. We can find it and we can split the take."

Slocum saw Gunnison feverishly reloading his rifle. When the magazine was again full, Gunnison called out, "How do I know I kin trust you this time?" He lifted the rifle and aimed into the darkness below. "Come on out and let's talk."

"That's a good idea," Clarke said.

Below Slocum saw movement. Gunnison instantly twisted

and began firing, but Clarke had decoyed him with his coat and hat on a stick. From several feet to the side of the lure came foot-long lances of fire leaping from Clarke's six-shooter.

Neither man had a good shot, but Slocum knew he had to act now.

"Hey, Gunnison! Up here!"

Startled, the outlaw turned, looked up, and spotted Slocum. He tried to get his long gun pointed at the new target. Slocum squeezed off three rounds. Each hit Gunnison smack in the chest. The man made a strange chuffing sound, sat down, dropped his rifle, and then tumbled over the edge of the rock where he had lain in ambush. His body tumbled down and came to rest a few feet to the side of the mine entrance.

"You hit, Gunnison? You're not playin' possum, are you?"

Slocum flattened himself as Clarke advanced, six-gun aimed at the body. When he came within ten feet, he fired smack into Gunnison. For a moment, Clarke stood stock-still, then he let out a whoop of glee.

"I got you this time, you stupid son of a bitch! That'll teach you to cross me!"

Clarke did a war dance around, then edged closer to verify that his former partner was dead. He kicked him a couple times, then rolled him over. Slocum couldn't see what Clarke did, then he realized the outlaw searched the dead man's pockets.

"You don't have any more on you than the last time I left you for dead," Clarke said. He stepped away to reload. Slocum tried to get a good shot, but the rock ledge Gunnison had tumbled from prevented it. When Clarke walked back to where he searched for the map Atkins had left, Slocum lowered his six-shooter. Let the outlaw find the map.

From everything that he had overheard, it seemed that the bailiff had somehow learned where Atkins hid a map showing the location of the silver from the robbery. Atkins might have used this to bribe the bailiff, but why the court officer would bring Clarke in as a partner wasn't something Slocum wanted to dwell on overmuch. He made his way down the side of the hill and came up on Clarke from behind the pile of spent ore. The dross not only hid his approach but also muffled his footsteps. In the dark he couldn't walk as silently as he would have liked.

Clarke cursed and then stopped suddenly, putting Slocum on guard. Slocum edged around to get a better look. Kneeling not ten yards away, Clarke gripped a large rock and rocked it back and forth a few times, then dislodged it.

"Found you, you son of a bitch." He leaned down and his arm disappeared into a hole until his shoulder pressed into the ground. Slocum straightened and moved out of hiding, coming up behind Clarke. The outlaw strained to get his hand down even deeper into the hole.

Slocum lifted his pistol to cover Clarke but stumbled and fell backward, sitting down hard. The ground rumbled and a distant rushing sounded, like a river flowing. But that couldn't be. This was the Sonoran Desert.

Clarke let out a cry of pain and surprise. Slocum struggled to lift his six-shooter, but the ground continued to shake and shiver under him. Then it fell away, taking Clarke with it. Slocum scrambled like an upside-down spider to get away from the crumbling edge of a pit. He pressed against the depleted ore pile before the ground stopped shaking and falling in on itself.

He tried to figure what had happened. It was as if the earth had just opened up and swallowed Clarke.

Slocum got his feet under him and made sure the ground was firm before he edged forward to the rim of the suddenly formed hole.

At the bottom lay Clarke, stirring and moaning. In his hand he held a small cylinder like a baking powder tin.

"I . . . I'm trapped. Help me!"

Slocum looked around, then realized Clarke was appealing to him. He laughed harshly.

"I plugged your worthless partner. Why shouldn't I leave you down there?"

"Gunnison? I shot him. He tried to ambush me, the son of a bitch." Clarke got to his knees. Water began filling the deep pit. He started dancing about, yelping. "It's hot!"

Slocum tried to figure out what had happened. He knew that to the west, the San Pedro River disappeared underground for long stretches, only to reappear. A bosque followed its course the entire distance. He saw no unusual vegetation putting its roots down into an underground river here, though. It might be too rocky, but Slocum couldn't say for certain.

"Slocum, please. I'm burning up!"

"Burn in hell."

"I can share the silver. I got Atkins's map. He hid his share. We can split it, me and you. It's yours, if you'll get me out!"

Slocum backed from the pit and started walking toward the cabin. From there he could get his bearings, find his horse, and get out of Arizona Territory. Every step he took made this resolve firmer and the decision seem better. Before he reached the cabin, he heard Clarke's piteous screams.

He backtracked and saw Clarke struggling in the mud, trying to get out. The water was waist-deep around him now. From the way he moved, he was being tortured by the hot water.

Clarke looked up and pleaded, "Get me out, and it'll all be yours. All of it. My life's worth more than any silver."

He held up the baking powder can as if this were the silver. Slocum saw that the water wasn't rising as fast now, but Clarke was up to mid-chest in it. He struggled to keep his footing.

"Please, Slocum, I can't swim."

"Did you get Gunnison's share? You tried to kill him. I got that much out of him ambushing you."

"I thought I did, but where he said he'd hid his share there wasn't nuthin'! Atkins musta taken it. It must all be here!" He shook the can again. From the way he clung to it, Slocum knew something important had to be inside. Clarke would go to his death grasping the can.

"Don't die yet," Slocum said. He turned and left the rim of the sinkhole, shutting out Clarke's cries for mercy. He rode his horse back, unfastened the rope from his saddle, and tossed the loop down to Clarke.

The outlaw didn't need to be told what to do with it. He snaked his way so the loop circled his body. By the time he was ready, Slocum had secured the rope around his saddle horn. The mare began backing away, just as if they had a calf on the other end. For a moment Slocum wondered if he was pulling dead weight. Then came a lewd sucking noise as Clarke's feet cleared from the muck. The man tumbled over the edge of the hole, panting for breath.

He still held the baking powder tin.

"Let me have the can."

"No!" Clarke clutched it to his mud-caked chest as if it were a small child needing protection by its mama.

"I won't throw you back in."

"You'll kill me the minute you get the map."

"I could do that right now," Slocum said, drawing his six-gun.

"I'll drop it!" Clarke stepped back to the edge of the sinkhole and held the can out.

Slocum put his heels to his horse. The mare backed up a few more feet, dragging Clarke away.

"We'll find this little treasure together, but you're my prisoner," Slocum said. Reluctantly Clarke passed over the can.

Slocum took it and felt a measure of revenge—even more than when he had plugged Gunnison. He was hitting the outlaw where it hurt the most, taking the silver he had killed to steal.

16

"Which is the top of the map?" Slocum turned it in a full circle. He couldn't make head nor tail from it. "Is there something more?"

"Let me see it." Clarke held out his hand. Slocum had left his rope coiled around the outlaw's middle. If Clarke tried anything, it wouldn't take much effort to yank him out of the saddle. Slocum reluctantly gave the map to him.

Clarke frowned as he peered at the map, then held it above his head, as if the sky would form a decent background. Finally returning it to a flat position in front of him, pressing the paper against his horse's neck, Clarke pointed. "There's a landmark. It's got to be the Tombstone courthouse."

"It's a cross. It might mean the town cemetery."

"Atkins didn't cotton much to cemeteries. He was downright scared of haints."

"That'd be a good place to hide your loot," Slocum said. "Greed always trumps fear."

Clarke laughed bitterly. "You don't know Atkins. He kept everything about himself in little boxes. He'd open one and he'd be as sweet to his wife as could be. Another lid

154

was pulled open and he could kill without thinking twice. When it came to planning robberies, well, he was 'bout the best there was."

"What made him so special?" Slocum craned his neck to get a better look at the map. Atkins knew what it meant, but why had he drawn a map at all? Slow Joe probably needed a map to find his spurs, but from all accounts Russ Atkins was a clever man. He had drawn this map to confuse, perhaps, but more likely to be used as collateral for something.

The bailiff was supposed to run the claim for the Silver Chalice through without a hitch. When Autumn killed Judge Alvarez, that panicked everyone in the courthouse. Judge Watkins would decide, but how he came to his decision probably had less to do with previous bribes than it did with saving his own hide. The bailiff, though, might have a second part to the map telling how to orient it.

Atkins could have used his portion of the map to insure the bailiff delivered on steering Watkins in the right direction. Slocum had seen the ore from the Silver Chalice and knew the mine was wildly profitable. Atkins could easily have made the decision to swap a few bags of silver for outright ownership.

"You killed him? Atkins?"

Clarke looked up, startled at the question. His mouth opened, then snapped shut.

"Gunnison did it. He was as untrustworthy as they come. Should never have partnered up with him, but he drifted into town one day and knew some of the right people. I thought he was all right."

"Atkins must have, too, since he set you both up with the robbery. Where did Slow Joe come in?"

"Atkins knew him. Don't know how and don't rightly care. Slow Joe probably owed him money, and this was an easy way to collect. Joe'd have to work mucking stalls for the rest of his life to make a dollar." He tapped the side of his head to show what he thought about his former partner.

Slocum had to remind himself Clarke and Gunnison had double-crossed Slow Joe, thinking to steal his share from the robbery. They hadn't known that Slocum had beaten them to it.

"This has to be it. He buried the silver somewhere south of town."

Slocum sat a little straighter in the saddle and wondered if this might be a map to where he had hidden the silver after taking it from Joe. He didn't see any way Atkins or the other robbers could have figured out where he had buried it. Unlike them, he didn't make maps and had not mentioned it to anyone. The marshal considered him one of the robbers, but that was Autumn's doing, and he had never told the woman what he had done. She had played on the recent robbery to remove him from the game she played, as if she thought he might become a contender for the Silver Chalice. More likely, she had realized he would not be bound slavishly to her for much longer. He was too restless and too sensible to let any woman corral him the way Autumn tried.

"Do you think Autumn is mixed up in this?"

"Of course she is. That bitch has her claws into everything that goes on. She's like a spider in a web, waiting and watching. She doesn't kill anything herself. She waits for her prey to get tangled up in a web—and it doesn't even have to be her web."

Clarke thrust the map out in front of him.

"This is it. See the wiggly line? That's got to be the Dragoon Mountains yonder. With it all lined up proper, we ride south of town."

"Not through town," Slocum warned. "I don't think either of us would receive a hospitable greeting there."

"The marshal's got it in for me, that's true," Clarke said. "By this time, the bailiff probably thinks I'm cheating him, too. The judge would issue an arrest warrant on his say-so.

I declare, that man's as bad as Autumn Dupree when it comes to meddling in town business."

They rode at an angle, missing even the outskirts of Tombstone by a mile or more. Still, Slocum felt edgy. The marshal looked to be a man who carried a grudge. Slocum kept glancing over his shoulder in the direction of the road leading into Tombstone, and this proved his downfall.

Clarke unwound the rope from his waist and used it as a lash to strike Slocum across the face. The rough hemp cut deep. The explosion of blood from the wound meant less to Slocum than the surprise. He flailed about for a moment, giving Clarke time to swing the rope a second time.

This wrapped around Slocum's neck. Clarke yanked, and Slocum flew from the saddle, hitting the ground hard enough to stun him. He blinked through blurred eyes and saw his horse galloping away.

He grunted and worked to get his six-shooter from its holster. Clarke paused a moment, obviously considering his chances against a dismounted Slocum, and then followed the right trail. He let out a *yip!* and sent his horse racing southward into the desert.

Slocum finally dragged his six-shooter from the holster and raised it. His eyes were still fogged from the fall, but he got off a shot. He had no idea if he came close to Clarke. Then he sank to all fours and panted like a dog to get his wind back. When he had finally cleared his head, he stood and touched his cheek. The rope had cut to the bone. Cursing under his breath, he awkwardly fastened his bandanna around his head to stanch the flow. When this didn't work, he simply pressed the cloth hard into the wound and began walking.

If he'd had the sense God gave a goose, he would have retrieved his horse, found his stash of silver, and ridden the hell out of Arizona Territory. Anger burned away common sense.

He topped a rise and squinted into the distance. The faint dust cloud marked his escaped prisoner's path. Whether Clarke had deciphered the map and made a beeline for Atkins's silver or if he simply rode to put as much distance between himself and Slocum as possible didn't matter. He would pay for this. To Slocum the silver became less important by the minute. Those he had on his list to even the score with diminished day by day. Gunnison and Atkins were dead. Clarke would be soon enough.

What he would do to Summer Lorritsen was something he thought long and hard on as he went after his horse.

Twenty minutes later he once more rode the trail, this time after Clarke. And he still hadn't decided on a fitting way of getting even with Summer and Autumn. They had both used him. He had taken some small pleasure with them, but it hardly compensated for being wanted for a robbery he didn't commit and who knows what else?

As he had hoped, Clarke wasn't too savvy about how hard to push his horse in the desert heat. Galloping for any distance wore down even the strongest horse. Without a decent watering hole to refresh and rejuvenate before pressing on, Clarke's mistreatment of the animal made it increasingly easy for Slocum to creep ever closer.

Even with a stronger mount, better horse sense, and a decent trail to follow, Slocum found himself faced with twilight. Tracking after dark was too difficult since Clarke had zigzagged as he rode, whether to throw Slocum off his trail or simply because he wasn't sure where he headed didn't matter. If Slocum missed one of the sharp turns the outlaw took, he would miss him entirely.

Settling down as the heat disappeared and was replaced by the cold, Slocum found himself a suitable spot for a camp. He considered a fire, then decided it might alert Clarke to how close pursuit had come. Having polished off a can of beans and some jerky that didn't have too many maggots in it, he finally lay back and stared at the stars. Tiny wisps of cloud that looked like smoke drifted across the sky, turning familiar constellations into something exotic. Slocum drifted off to sleep making new patterns.

He came awake with a start when a distant gunshot rolled across the endless desert. His six-shooter came easily to hand as he waited for a second shot that never came. He slowly returned his Colt to its holster and stood. He sniffed the air hard to catch any scent of a campfire. Nothing reached his sensitive nose.

He walked some distance from his camp, straining every sense to locate the gunshot. The single shot had died away, never to be tracked. Slocum gauged his chances, decided on the general direction of the shot, and saddled his tired horse, amid loud equine protests. A few pats on the neck and some encouraging words got the horse moving along at a slow walk.

Guesswork kept him on the trail. As he rode slowly, he listened hard and was glad he did so. It saved his life. Movement some distance to his right caused him to bend low as a bullet seared through the space where his head had been only an instant before. Slocum slid off the horse and let it bolt. As tired as the mare was, she wouldn't run far.

Slocum drew his six-shooter and began stalking the unseen sniper. For more than a half hour he worked his way in the direction of the shot, but he found nothing. In the darkness he might have missed the evidence—he probably had. He hadn't heard the sniper ride away, but no one was around to continue the fight with him. Reluctantly, he returned to the spot where he had let his horse run free, and quickly found the mare only a dozen yards away.

On foot, leading his horse, he explored the area and found Clarke's cold camp. The outlaw's horse was nowhere to be seen, but his gear had been stretched out and the man had sprawled on it, using the saddle as a pillow. Slocum advanced, his six-gun cocked and ready, but he knew instinctively his caution wasn't needed.

Clarke was dead.

When he stood over the man, he saw that Clarke had been shot squarely in the head. Either the sniper had made one hell of a shot or he had been close enough to get a decent sight picture. Slocum thrust the toe of his boot under Clarke and heaved. The man rolled over awkwardly. The bullet had gone clean through Clarke's head and embedded in the saddle.

Slocum knelt, rolled Clarke onto his back again, and methodically searched him. Everything the outlaw had carried in his pockets was gone—including the map he claimed Atkins had planted back at the Silver Chalice mine.

It took less than a minute for Slocum to make another circuit of the camp. Whoever had shot the outlaw was long gone by now. And why not? Clarke had been killed for the map. Slocum was sure of that. What he wasn't as sure about was the identity of the outlaw's killer.

Clarke claimed to have killed most everyone who would be interested in the map. Atkins was probably dead, Gunnison certainly was. Slow Joe was a casualty of the robbery at the hands of his partners. Who had killed Clarke?

Slocum decided it didn't matter. The map to where Atkins had hidden his share of the silver was gone. He settled down on a rock and stared at the body for a few minutes, working on his best course of action. Then he got to work burying Clarke's body, cursing himself for an idiot the entire while.

He ought to be on the trail to California or Nevada or even Texas. The farther he rode from Arizona Territory the better. All he had to do to show a tidy profit was to retrieve the silver from the stolen shipment and be on his way.

He ought to ride hard and long and fast. Instead, he headed back toward Tombstone at first light.

17

Slocum heard gunfire before he reached the city limits. He slowed and looked around, worrying that the ruckus would bring the marshal running. Where the shots had been fired he could not tell, but they came from ahead. Veering away, Slocum headed for the far end of Tombstone, keeping the courthouse in sight as he rode. The entire way back he had thought on who had killed Clarke. There seemed only one reasonable answer, and he worked in the courthouse.

The bailiff had his finger in about every pie and certainly had more power than was obvious. He controlled what and when the judges saw cases, and he could be bribed. That was a combination that suggested to Slocum that the bailiff had known about Atkins's map—it had probably been intended as a bribe. If Atkins gained control of the Silver Chalice, what were a couple paltry bags of silver planchets? Atkins would be rich whether he sold the mine or worked it himself. Even better from Atkins's point of view, he would be out from under the onus of the silver robbery that had left two well-known and -liked citizens of Tombstone dead.

Planning the robbery was both safer and more profitable than committing it.

Especially when all your henchmen ended up dead and you had stolen their loot.

More gunfire from along Fremont Street steered Slocum south of town, following a dirt path running parallel to the Good Enough Mine road. He came up to the courthouse and rode around it once, keen eyes hunting for activity inside. It was late enough in the afternoon, and hot enough to boot, to have emptied the building in favor of a saloon.

A couple horses were tethered behind the courthouse. Otherwise, Slocum saw no sign that anyone remained within. He added his horse to the other pair, then walked on cat's feet up the back steps. He drew his pistol and used the barrel to push open the door so he could see down a long corridor to the foyer. The building settled, giving him a chorus of creaks and moans as the wood dried out in the sun. Other than this, he heard nothing.

But two horses meant two men were somewhere in the building.

Walking down the corridor, testing each step before he put his weight on it to keep a creaky floor from announcing his arrival, Slocum finally reached the foyer. Stairs to his right led up to the second floor. All the doors off the foyer stood open, but no voices came out from the rooms beyond. To his right lay the judge's chambers and the courtroom where he had seen the opening argument between the two sisters over ownership of the Silver Chalice.

A solitary closed door with frosted glass in it drew him. The bailiff's office was as quiet as the rest of the building. Slocum turned the doorknob slowly. Unlocked. He took a deep breath, then opened the door fast and slid inside, six-shooter aimed and ready.

He pointed his gun at a body sprawled across the desk. Judging from the way the blotter under the man's head was soaked with blood, there wasn't a whole lot of chance the bailiff was still alive. Slocum pressed his fingers into the man's neck just under his muttonchop whiskers. He didn't find a pulse, but he already knew the bailiff was dead from the clammy feel of his skin and the puffiness of the flesh. The man had been dead for some time.

Quickly searching the man's pockets yielded nothing. Slocum poked through the bailiff's desk drawers, then worked on the files hunting for anything that would be of value to him. He more or less remembered the map Atkins had been killed carrying. In spite of what Clarke had told Slocum, a second part to the map was needed to locate where Atkins had hidden the silver from the robbery. If it had played out the way Slocum thought, at least half the remaining silver was buried under the X on the map.

If the bailiff had a key to the map, it was gone along with his killer. Slocum looked around but saw nothing of interest. As he entered the foyer, he saw a deputy outside walking resolutely toward the front steps. The man had his head down, swung his arms as if he could propel himself a little faster this way, and took the front steps two at a time in his haste to enter the courthouse.

Slocum started to get the drop on the lawman, then ducked into the courtroom instead. Two horses out back. One probably belonged to the bailiff. That meant someone else was in the building. He peered out as the deputy never slowed as he made his way down the corridor leading out back.

Slocum followed him a ways and watched. The second horse belonged to the deputy. He started to mount, then stopped. He scratched his chin, then went to Slocum's mare and gentled the animal, studying it from every side before coming back around. He frowned and looked at the horse, then up the back steps. Slocum ducked into the foyer to avoid being seen.

He heard the deputy reenter the corridor. His boot heels clicked on the wood floor as he returned. From his vantage, Slocum watched the deputy slowly look around. Like a magnet drawn to iron, the deputy went to the bailiff's office door and rapped sharply on the glass with his knuckle.

"Hey, Desmond, you got a visitor? There's another horse out back. Been rode hard and wasn't there a few minutes ago. Desmond? Stop yer sleepin' and answer me."

The deputy opened the office door and stuck his head in. Slocum took the chance and hurried down the corridor as the deputy let out a yelp of surprise and then cursed when he found the dead bailiff. It took a couple seconds, but Slocum grabbed the reins of the other two horses and mounted. He rode slowly, not wanting to kick up a fuss, until he got to a trail leading southward into the desert.

"Giddyap!" He chased off the two horses. The one belonged to the deputy and the other was probably the bailiff's. It would take the lawman a few minutes to figure out what to do. He might go fetch the marshal or he might squeal like a stuck pig over losing his horse. Whatever he did would give Slocum a few more minutes to disappear from Tombstone. Nothing but dead bodies lay along his trail, and he did what he should have done days earlier.

He hunted for the spot where he had buried the silver, with the avowed intent of taking it as far into Mexico as he could ride.

After an exhausting day he stood over his treasure. The silver gleamed in the setting sun since he had opened the bag to be certain the slugs were still there. As far as Slocum could tell, no one had disturbed his loot. But staring at it, bending down and running his fingers through it, erased some of the resolve that had built on his way from Tombstone. It made no sense to get revenge on Autumn and Summer, but he had to. Both had done him dirty. Worse, they had used him—though in a most pleasurable way. Nobody but them would ever know.

Nobody but the sisters and himself.

Slocum scooped the slugs back into the bag and hefted it. Two bags filled with the silver would serve him well for a long time. It didn't matter that he would never get the rest of the stolen shipment, but a tiny knot of curiosity began to chafe and worry at him. Someone had killed Atkins and the bailiff. The only ones who could know of the silver shipment had to be Summer and Autumn. One of them might have found out from Atkins. It wasn't out of the question that the half map Atkins had buried at the Silver Chalice, the one that Clarke had retrieved, had been intended as payoff to the sisters in exchange for the mine. How that deal could ever have been legal—or how Atkins could have believed the two would ever play square with him—added to the questions burning in Slocum's brain.

He slung the silver over his mare's rump and secured it to his saddlebags, mounted, and for a moment faced south. Mexico. It was only a few days' ride, and he would be away from this crazy double-crossing and back-shooting.

Tugging on his horse's reins, he wheeled about and cut across country toward the Silver Chalice. A little after dawn, he realized how big a mistake he had made. In the distance off to his left rose a dust cloud. Only a small herd of horses could have kicked so much up. He watched as it moved along the horizon at the pace of a horse's trot.

"Posse," he said to himself. His mare twisted her head around and fixed a big brown eye on him, as if accusing him of being the world's stupidest rider. Slocum wasn't going to argue the point. He could still head for Mexico. And then he knew it was too late for that.

A rider topped a rise not a quarter mile away. For a heartbeat, the rider simply sat and stared in Slocum's direction. Then sunlight glinted off a spyglass. Before Slocum could let out the breath he had caught and held, the rider vanished behind the ridge.

The posse's scout had spotted him. Slocum looked around for a hiding place. Outrunning the posse wasn't likely to be possible. They rode fresh horses. His mare had valiantly carried him without much to eat and damned little to drink

over the past week. For the first time he wished he had kept
the two horses he had taken at the rear of the courthouse.
Riding one until it tired, then switching to the next until it,
too, tired would have let him put fifty miles a day behind
him.

He snapped the reins and dropped down into a broad,
shallow arroyo. This got him out of the direct line of sight,
but if the scout reported with enough sincerity about what
he had seen, the marshal was sure to come investigate. Riding slowly, conserving both his and his horse's strength, Slocum continued in the direction of the Silver Chalice. The
posse might think he'd hightail it straight for Mexico. If
they tried to cut him off, they'd pass him by entirely.

"You sure you saw that varmint?" The marshal's irasci-
ble growl was distinctive, even at a distance. Slocum drew
rein and waited. The arroyo didn't provide much cover, but
it was better than nothing. If he silhouetted himself against
the sky, he was a goner.

"Sure as can be, Marshal," the scout said in a loud voice,
as if this would convince the lawman more than his tracking skills. "I seen him drinkin' in the Birdcage Saloon plain
as day. Has to be the same fellow."

Slocum frowned. He had been out in the desert getting
himself shot at and doing all he could to avoid being seen.

"Nobody guns down two men in my town and gets away
with it."

Slocum wondered if the posse was on the trail of the
gunman responsible for the ruckus he'd heard when he had
sneaked back to the courthouse. It hardly mattered who the
posse caught—either him or the cowboy responsible for shooting up a saloon and a couple patrons would be a fine day's
catch for the marshal.

"You think he killed Desmond, too?"

"Who the hell knows? You men, fan out. Spread out
along a quarter-mile search area. Don't get out of sight of

the man on either side of you. I don't want him gettin' away, you hear me?"

A chorus of agreement rose. Slocum kept moving along the arroyo, then dismounted and pressed close to the three-foot-high embankment. The raging summer runoff had cut a vertical bank, but it wasn't tall enough to hide his horse, too. Realizing this, Slocum fastened the reins around a rock and made his way a few yards down the dry riverbed. He began digging like a berserk gopher until he had a shallow depression in the dried wall. Turning around, he pressed his back into it and drew his Colt.

He couldn't stand off the entire posse, but he could take one or two of them with him.

In less than a minute of improvising his hiding place, he heard the soft thudding of a horse's hooves above his head. The rider was headed away from the spot down the arroyo where Slocum had left his horse.

"You boys seein' any sign of 'im?" The marshal's bellow could be heard halfway back to Tombstone.

Slocum jumped a foot when a rider burst from the undergrowth on the far side of the arroyo. The man kept low, but Slocum got a decent look at him. He wore a black cloth cutaway coat and sported a bowler pulled down squarely so his ears pressed against the brim. His hands glinted in the sunlight from a half dozen rings.

"There he goes! It's him. The one what shot up the saloon! After him, men. Be careful. He's already killed two men!"

The rider above him sent a cascade of dirt and rock onto Slocum's head. Slocum ducked and then the air filled with a leaping horse. The deputy raced across the arroyo, up the far bank, and finally dragged out his six-gun. A few wild shots drew the rest of the posse's attention. At several paces away from where Slocum hid, riders crashed down into the arroyo and struggled up the far bank. Within minutes, the sound of their hoofbeats had died off.

Slocum sank down and shook in relief. Only then did
he realize how keyed up he had been. He returned his six-
shooter to his holster and decided it was about time Lady
Luck smiled on him after all that he had been through. The
gambler had saved his hide as surely as if the earth had
opened up and swallowed the entire posse, marshal and all.

He made his way back to where his horse nibbled at
mesquite beans on a branch dangling down from the arroyo
rim. Slocum tugged on the reins and got the mare moving.
He didn't want to mount and ride, not yet. Let the posse put
another mile between them. Then he'd feel safer.

"Hey, which way'd they go?"

Slocum's hands started for his pistol, but he caught himself. He glanced over his saddle at the arroyo's rim where a
youngster, hardly fifteen from the way he looked, stood in
the stirrups, straining to find the posse.

"Due south."

"How come you're not ridin' with 'em?" The youngster
fingered a rifle sheathed at his knee.

"Horse pulled up lame. Might be a rock under the shoe.
Need to get out of this pit and check."

"I help my uncle shoe horses. Want me to take a look for
you?"

"You go on, catch up with the rest of 'em," Slocum said,
trying not to sound too nervous. He didn't want to kill this
youngster, but he knew if it came down to gunplay, that's
the way any fight would end.

"Can't just strand you here."

"If you're not there when they catch that murdering
gambler, you don't get a share of the reward," Slocum said.

"I won't? That's not what the marshal said back in
town."

"That's the way it is. I'll be all right. You go on and
catch up."

"I sorely do need the money," the boy said. "All right,

mister, but I'll stop by again when we take that murderin' dog back to town and see how you're farin'."

"Thanks. Appreciate it."

Slocum heaved a sigh of relief as the boy trotted across the sandy spit, up the far bank, and disappeared. His luck still ran true. Or maybe it was the boy's luck that had saved him. Slocum mounted and headed back in the direction of the road out of Tombstone that led to the Silver Chalice Mine. With the law after the gambler, they wouldn't be prowling in this direction. When they caught the gambler, they'd probably take him back to Tombstone for a proper hanging since there weren't trees tall enough in this part of the desert.

Slocum silently wished the gambler well, hoping that the posse had to chase him for a good, long time.

When he came to the turnoff leading to the silver mine, he considered forgetting about the sisters and their deadly squabble over the Silver Chalice. For all he knew, the man who had died wasn't even their pa. But too many others had died as a result of their feud. Slocum wasn't sure what he could do to put an end to it short of shooting both women, but that wasn't out of the question after what they'd done to him.

He reached the base of the hill where the mine stuck out like a sore thumb. The pile of drossy rock looked a bit lower to him, making him wonder if the sinkhole that had opened and swallowed Clarke wasn't slowly devouring everything around.

Voices in the distance caused Slocum to pause, his hand resting on the ebony handle of his six-shooter. Two people argued—both women. He couldn't make out the words, but there wasn't any friendliness to this discussion. Slocum imagined both women pressed nose to nose shouting at each other. With such passion, it wouldn't take them long to come to blows.

If they killed each other, that would probably satisfy his need for revenge, since it would be so well-deserved on both their parts. It seemed fitting that each would be the other's nemesis. If they didn't, he might figure out some way for them both to lose this claim. Depriving them of the Silver Chalice would be far worse punishment than killing them outright, he had decided on his way up from the main road.

"Take away what they want the most and be sure they can never get it." Slocum wasn't sure how that could be done, but the fake will—if it was bogus—might be part of the solution. Whatever he did had to be done as secretly as possible. If he showed his face in Tombstone, he was likely to hang beside the gambler before the day was out.

Whatever he could find could be turned to his advantage. Wasn't luck riding on his shoulder now?

Slocum rode slowly closer to the mine, hunting for Summer and Autumn. He caught a glimpse of them from the corner of his eye. Both stood near the mouth of the mine. As he studied the terrain more closely, he was startled to see how much work had been done to reopen the mine. Most of the mouth had been clogged with rock and debris from when he had escaped the cave-in brought about by Gunnison's dynamite.

One of them had gotten the mine ready to return to full production. From the last he had heard, it was likely to have been Autumn's doing. Summer still tried to maneuver her sister in court, but Slocum thought Autumn had the edge there and would likely keep the mine since she didn't care who she slept with.

One woman shoved the other. Then a donnybrook started, with hair-pulling, shouting, and fists flying.

Slocum looped one leg around his pommel, leaned forward, and enjoyed the fight.

The bullet from behind took him out of the saddle and sent him crashing to the ground.

18

Slocum's horse reared and then galloped away, leaving him on the ground. He lay with his arms pulled in close to his sides so he could keep his six-shooter within easy reach. Playing possum was a dangerous tactic, but he had no other choice. He hadn't intended to fall off his horse the way he had, but the bullet had driven through his hat and grazed the side of his head. The lightning bolt of pain had stunned him. Just enough.

Knowing he was exposed to the sniper, he gathered his strength, got his wits about him, and doubted his wound was serious. His vision wasn't blurred, and his arms and legs felt strong. He tested them instantly, rolling to hands and knees, then digging in his toes and rocketing forward. He hit the ground and skidded a few feet so he landed behind the depleted ore pile. New slugs sang through the air, but he was safe—for the moment. He had guessed the location of the sniper accurately. Now it was up to him to put that knowledge to some use.

Slocum drew his pistol, glanced in the direction of the mine, but didn't see either Summer or Autumn, then climbed the heap of dross until he could sneak a quick peek over the top, where the sniper would least expect him.

In a flash he took in the situation. The dry-gulcher hid behind the corner of the cabin. At this range all Slocum could hope for was to pin the sniper down. Hitting him using only a handgun would be more luck than skill. It never paid to attempt to outshoot a man with a rifle when the distance was this great.

He slid back down the slope, kicked away bits of stone from his knees and hands, then worked out his plan. Rather than think about it, Slocum simply acted. Ten quick steps took him to the lip of the sinkhole where Clarke had been swallowed up. He spun, dropped onto his belly, and slid down a few feet. He dug his toes in and prevented the plunge all the way to the bottom of the water-filled hole. From this position he painstakingly worked his way back to the top of the hole and saw his target.

The sniper had lost track of him. From his new vantage point, Slocum had an angle he had lacked before. He sighted in carefully, then squeezed off a shot. It went low but nicked the sniper in the leg. The man yelped, whirled around, and frantically sought whoever had shot him. Slocum got off a second round before the man twigged to his mistake. Slocum was no longer behind the mine tailings but had gotten a better position.

He raised his rifle as Slocum shot a third time. The range was extreme for a handgun, but he tore off a hunk of wall beside the man's face. A splinter ripped through his cheek, making him flinch just as he fired another round.

Slocum fired again, but the sniper had had enough and ran for all he was worth.

A quick look in the direction of the mine failed to reveal the two women. They might have ducked inside once the shooting began. About all Slocum knew for a fact was that neither Autumn nor Summer had taken the shots at him.

The sisters wouldn't go anywhere. He wanted to know who had ambushed him.

Slocum ran to the near side of the cabin and carefully looked around the side. He knew the sniper had lit out, but he could have doubled back. If Slocum had been the one drawing the bead, this is what he would have done. Advancing cautiously, he found the trail where freshly broken bits of greasewood pointed the way as if the man had purposefully wanted Slocum to follow.

This thought turned Slocum even more cautious. He got off the game trail and worked his way downhill to the spot where the sniper had left his horse. Tracks led off to another game trail that seemed to curl back in the direction of the mine.

Slocum felt a sudden sinking sensation. He cursed and ran back to the cabin. He rounded the side in time to see a man bent low over his horse galloping away.

Not caring where the women were, Slocum got to his horse and saw that the trick had worked too well. He had blundered after someone who knew the lay of the land better than he ever could. The bags holding the silver slugs were missing. Slocum shouted in anger, then settled down.

"He's not going to keep them for long," he said as he thrust his foot into the stirrup and tried to step up. The saddle rotated around the mare and came crashing down atop Slocum as he lay on the ground. He cursed some more, then examined the cinch strap. It hadn't been cut, but the sniper had loosened it. By the time Slocum cinched it down tight enough to ride, he knew the silver thief was likely a mile or two away.

He still had to go after the man. Reaching the road back to Tombstone, Slocum looked in both directions and cursed some more.

Dust devils danced along the road either way, covering

any dirt kicked up by a fleeing horse's hooves. The oppressively hot air crushed down on him and made him even angrier. Slocum rode in the direction of town, vowing to take back his silver even if he had to fight off the marshal, all his deputies, and the rest of the town. He topped a rise in the road and got a good look for the next several miles.

The Arizona Territory desert was barren. So was the road leading into Tombstone. The sniper had ridden in the other direction. Or maybe he had found himself a hiding place and just let Slocum rush past. By now the man who had stolen the silver Slocum had taken from Slow Joe could be anywhere.

With that thought, Slocum twisted about to study his backtrail again. The sniper had a fine shot with Slocum silhouetted against the sky. But the road behind was as empty as the desert in all the other directions. Even the dust devils had died down, too exhausted to continue their mindless spinning in the gathering heat.

With a last look in the direction of Tombstone and still seeing no hint of human movement, Slocum turned his mare's face and headed back to the Silver Chalice. He considered riding a mile or two along the road going east to see if he could catch sight of the sniper, but he knew by now the man was long gone. If he had a lick of sense and realized who he had stolen the silver from, he would be in New Mexico by now.

Slocum tethered his horse in the shade beside the cabin and started for the mouth of the mine. Most all of the debris had been removed and new supports held the roof up. So much work couldn't have been done without assistance. Slocum wondered who the women had gotten to do it since he doubted they could have done it themselves, even if they worked together.

He went into a crouch, hand going for his six-shooter, when he heard a shot deep in the mine. Whoever had fired wasn't aiming at him. Slocum slipped just inside the mouth of the mine, looking up at the roof. Expert work had shored it up after Gunnison had dynamited it closed and Autumn had blown a bit more away. Slocum snorted. She had freed him only to use him. He would have taken the fall—literally—for robbing the silver shipment and killing the marshal's friends. And what little of the silver shipment he'd had was now missing.

Slocum was rapidly losing every good feeling he had for Arizona Territory and the two surviving sisters. First he would deal with them and then he would figure out how to recoup his loss of the silver.

More than once as he worked his way deeper into the mine, the idea cropped up that he could simply return the mouth to the condition it had been after Gunnison's handiwork. There had to be more dynamite around the camp. A few sticks, placed with better knowledge of how to do the job, and the Silver Chalice would be sealed forever.

It was all Summer and Autumn deserved, trapped with each other until they died. He suspected they'd be at each other like Kilkenny cats.

Slocum pressed against the mine wall when a slug came whining up from the dark depths. It smashed into a wood support and embedded there. He should have left then and there, but he was feeling ornery. He wanted as much from those two as he could get, no matter who owned this mine. There had to be a pile of silver around, and he deserved it for all his trouble.

More shots came from farther ahead, but he didn't have to dodge these slugs. They were fired into one of the drifts off to his right. The maze of digging had produced an incredible series of tunnels, some hardly wider than his shoulders and others opening into vaulted rooms. The Silver Chalice had been exploited—and there was so much more to dig from the walls.

Slocum took a miner's candle from a rock shelf and lit it. He stuffed a half dozen more candles in his pocket. If he played his cards right, only one woman would survive. Bartering with either Summer or Autumn might get him what he wanted.

The deeper he went into the mine, the more that tally of silver mounted. When the first candle had burned to a nubbin, he considered leaving the mine and letting the survivor, if there was one, come out to him. Tracking them in the darkness of the labyrinth was looking increasingly suicidal to him.

Just as he came to the sensible conclusion to leave the mine, he heard scuffling sounds ahead. He held the flickering candle at arm's length in his left hand as he drew his six-gun. If either of the sisters fired at the light, they'd miss him by a couple feet. He readied himself for the sharp report of their pistol and the foot-long orange fire spitting from the muzzle.

"John? Is that you, John?"

"Hello, Summer. Where's your sister?"

"She's trying to kill me. She thinks that will get her the mine. She doesn't know!"

"Know what?"

"I have all the legal papers together. The mine is in my name now, and if anything happens to me, I've willed it to Nellie Cashman."

"Who?" The name sounded familiar.

"She runs a hospital in Tombstone. She's about the only decent person in the entire territory," Summer said. Slocum remembered now. He had eaten at this woman's restaurant. Giving her the silver mine seemed a strange act of charity— Summer must think this was the ultimate insult to her sister.

"You won the judge over?"

"Yes," the woman said, her word sounding like a snake threatening to strike. "It didn't matter that Autumn killed Judge Alvarez to scare Watkins. I won him over in spite of that!"

"I didn't kill anybody!" The screech tore at Slocum's

ears. The sound built and echoed off every wall, making it impossible to tell where it came from.

"You murdered him. Who else would have done it?"

"Win did it. I swear, it was Win!"

"Winthrop?" Slocum wondered how that jackass had dealt himself into this game, yet he had been in the courtroom. Considering how many people had staked a claim on this piece of real estate, it probably wasn't too far-fetched that a no-account like Winthrop had tried to join in.

"He's a lazy, no good, son of a—"

"Bitch! Don't talk about him that way." Wherever Autumn hid, she had a shot at her sister. Slocum didn't see the muzzle flash, but the report deafened him. Summer ran for Slocum, arms outstretched. All she succeeded in doing was knocking the miner's candle from his grip. In an instant the stone room was plunged into utter darkness.

"John, please, I'll make you a partner. I'll do whatever you want. Anything," Summer said, her voice turning seductive. He knew exactly what she meant, but he had to get past her attempt to kill him. Not that bedding Autumn had been much better. Sharing her favors had been pleasurable, but being framed for two murders he hadn't committed had been a disagreeable portion of that liaison. The two sisters were pure poison.

"I want twenty pounds of silver. That's it. Give it to me, and I'll leave you be."

"She's going to kill me. Us! Stop her and the silver's yours. I promise. I have that much in the Tombstone bank. There's probably almost that much on its way from the smelter outside town from the last load of ore I sent."

"I'll give you double that," came Autumn's promise. "Kill her, John. She's going to double-cross you."

"Like she did! She told the marshal you—"

"I know what she did. And I know what you did, too. Both of you wanted me dead. Now I want to be paid for all my trouble."

"You will be, if you kill her for me," Summer said.

Slocum stepped away from her in the darkness. She thrashed around, trying to find him. He moved softly in the direction where he guessed Autumn had waited for her sister. Although he had given these stopes only a cursory examination before, he had a good idea where they led. The main shaft lay behind Autumn, putting her between him and escape.

"I want to help you, Autumn. You say you'll give me forty pounds of silver?"

"She's offering you twenty pounds of silver, you Judas! I'll give you forty."

Slocum marveled at how the two women could be locked in a death fight and still argue over payment. They were worse than sidewinders. A snake was an honest killer, true to its nature. Summer and Autumn shifted constantly, maneuvering for an advantage and not caring about the truth.

Instinct made Slocum crouch. He was dazzled by the muzzle blast not ten feet away, but the afterimage burning in his eyes showed him where Autumn stood. He lifted his pistol to fire. Then he froze.

"What's that noise?" he called out.

"Shoot her!"

Slocum wasn't even certain which of the sisters had spoken. He strained to hear a sound just beyond the limits of his hearing. Then he felt the rock floor shiver under his boots. A million things flashed through his mind, then it all came together.

"Clarke, he was sucked down into a sinkhole. Outside the mine."

"So what? She wants me dead, John." This was from Summer.

"Out of the mine. Run for it. We can't stay here a second longer."

Slocum bulled his way forward, wrapped his arms around Autumn, but released her when she fired her six-shooter.

The bullet ripped a crease in Slocum's upper thigh. It burned like hellfire, but he hardly noticed. He shook the woman hard.

"Get out of the mine. You and Summer have to leave now. Now!"

He released her, but Autumn no longer showed any interest in him. Her sister had lit a candle in the stony chamber. The two rushed for each other, clawing and fighting.

"The mine's going to flood. There's an underground river breaking through. The sinkhole was only the start." He shouted but couldn't make himself heard over their furious shrieks as they locked in combat.

Slocum took a step toward the two figures limned in the flickering light of the candle, then felt what was close to an earthquake. Dust formed a veil between him and the sisters.

Still, he had to get them out. He couldn't let two women, even conniving ones like Autumn and Summer, die in the mine. Then he had no choice. The dust turned to a steady curtain of rock tumbling down. Along with the loose stone came a spray of hot water. Slocum threw up his hand to protect his face and turned away. He needed a candle to see the way, but there wasn't time to light another. Working on instinct alone, he found the main shaft. In the distance shone a tiny spot—the mouth of the mine and the Arizona desert beyond.

He ran. Hard. His feet pounded against the floor and he slipped in the loose stone and dust, but he focused on making the tiny spot of light grow. And it did, but from the depths of the mine came a belching noise as if some giant had eaten something that didn't agree with him. Then hot water engulfed Slocum, and the mine gave out a bone-chilling death cry as it fell in on itself.

19

Slocum tried to get his feet under him, but the force at his back proved too powerful. He fought, twisting and turning, then ran out of strength and allowed the water to drive him onward. He was battered against the roof and walls of the Silver Chalice and then exploded out into brilliant sunlight. He hit the ground, tumbled, and fell flat on his back in a sea of mud. He blinked his eyes clear and saw a torrent of water arching above him.

He rolled away from the sinkhole and made his way to the cabin. Wiping water from his face, he stared at the geyser erupting from the mouth of the mine. The sinkhole that had swallowed Clarke began to grow. The water from the mine devoured the earth and made the hole ever deeper. Slocum realized the water that had filled the hole before was only a small trickle compared to the actual underground river that had finally burst free of the mine.

He watched in awe as it continued to gush forth for several minutes before settling down to a steady trickle. Slocum took off his coat and vest and wrung them out the best he could. The water in his boots was poured out quickly enough, but all he could do for the rest of his clothing was to simply stand in the hot sunlight. It took only a few minutes before the cloth was stiff and plastered to his body, but he was generally dry. Only then did he walk back to the mine and peer in.

From the depths he heard the steady rush of water. Whether the mining had weakened the rock and let the subsurface river blast forth or the water would have chewed its way out eventually on its own hardly mattered. Both Autumn and Summer were down in the mine.

Sloshing through ankle-deep puddles, he reentered and took a candle from his coat pocket. Lighting it took a few minutes, but the waterproof tin holding his lucifers had kept out the worst of the moisture. The wick sputtered fitfully before giving enough light for him to work his way deeper into the mine. A few side chambers were already draining, but when he came to the passage leading to where he and the two sisters had been, Slocum knew they could not have survived.

The water was still chest-high and swirling forcefully. He had been battered about as the water shoved him from the mine. Neither of the women had gotten to the main shaft in time—they had been too busy trying to kill each other for that. The surge in this chamber would have crushed them instantly, not even giving them time to drown. Slocum wasn't sure if that was good or not.

He held the candle up high. The vortex in the middle of the room showed where the water drained, but somehow it entered at the same rate somewhere else. The candle smoked and flickered as the air began to turn bad. As he turned to leave, he saw what looked like bloody streaks high on the wall. Nearby was a long tattered strip of cloth. In the darkness he hadn't seen what either woman wore, but this could well be from a skirt. He didn't bother trying to pull it free. There wasn't any reason for him to take a souvenir from this watery grave.

Somehow, the distance out of the mine stretched for miles and miles. By the time Slocum wearily emerged, he felt as if he had fought a daylong battle. Every muscle in his body ached and more than a few cuts oozed fresh blood.

He went to the cabin and poked around, finding a bottle of whiskey with a few shots left in it. Some of the whiskey he used to clean his wounds. The final two shots he downed to kill the rest of his pain. Using Summer's petticoat taken from a drawer, he bound up the worst of his injuries. His head felt as if it were a rotted melon about ready to explode in the noonday sun. He lay back on the bed. As he drifted off to sleep, he remembered how he had passed some pleasant hours in this very bed. Now it felt hard, cold, and uninviting.

It was almost dawn when he awoke. He shook off the last gauzy veils of sleep and stood, moaning softly. He stretched, moved about, and finally got some feeling back in places where it had disappeared. By the time he had eaten what little food was in the larder, he felt almost human again.

He went outside and studied the mine. A tiny rivulet ran steadily from the mine into the sinkhole. Before he mounted to leave, Slocum filled his canteen from the new river and tasted the water. It had a bitter taste to it, but he had drunk worse. He let his mare drink her fill, then made sure she had adequate food before hitting the trail.

When he reached the road, he looked back at the hill where the Silver Chalice bored down into the rock. Common sense told him to ride in any direction but Tombstone. But one thing Autumn had said burned in his mind now. She had defended Winthrop. Maybe she had been using him as she had used Slocum and so many others, but it hadn't sounded that way. She had been genuinely angry with her sister over the insults heaped on Winthrop's head.

Summer would have left the mine to charity. Would Autumn have left it to Winthrop? Slocum decided he wanted this one last answer since he had nothing else to show for his time in Tombstone.

The ride to town went slowly. He didn't want to tire his horse, because if the marshal and his deputies were on the alert, he might have to race them away from town. But it was mid-afternoon and hotter than hell's furnace hinges when he rode down Allen Street. Anyone with good sense was inside, out of the direct sunlight. Several saloons blared music and occasionally a half-naked soiled dove appeared in an upstairs window, listlessly watching him. At least they were as cool as they possibly could be, even if business was slack.

Slocum drew rein and listened as he passed by a long, narrow saloon crammed between a dry goods store and a gun smithy. The booming, bragging voice guided him to the front doors and through them. At the bar, making the ruckus, stood Winthrop.

"I got the whole damned world by the tail," Winthrop declared, "and I'm gonna swing it round my head like a cat by the tail!"

Slocum made sure his six-gun rode easy in his holster. He had been through a considerable amount of trouble and wanted the wet leather to allow the weapon to slide easily. He had already cleaned the gun and reloaded. It was a reliable gun. It wouldn't fail him now.

"Another drink," Slocum said, indicating that the barkeep ought to give Winthrop another shot of rye.

"Much obliged. Glad somebody 'preciates me in this worthless town."

"Town's not as worthless as some of the lop-eared jack-asses in it," Slocum said.

"I gotta agree," Winthrop said, still not turning to see who had bought him the drink. "The marshal's a fool. And—" Something about the way the others at the bar had fallen silent warned Winthrop. He looked over his shoulder, saw Slocum, and went for his six-shooter.

Winthrop was too drunk to make a decent play. Slocum stepped forward, grabbed the scruff of his neck, and slammed his face down into the bar so hard the shot glass bounced straight up and crashed back. Somehow, the liquor wasn't spilled.

Slocum reached over Winthrop, still holding him by the back of the neck, took the whiskey, and knocked it back. He choked. The tarantula juice laced with nitric acid didn't have as much kick now. He slid it down to the barkeep and nodded when the man held up a bottle, silently inquiring if Slocum wanted another shot. He did.

After downing this, Slocum jerked Winthrop around and steered him toward a table at the rear of the saloon. Shoving him down, he lifted the man's six-gun in the same motion. Slocum laid the gun on the table between them. Winthrop looked from Slocum to the gun and back, trying to make up his mind what to do.

"Don't," Slocum advised.

"What do you want?"

"I've had some time to think about what happened at the Silver Chalice."

"It's mine! I got all the papers. The deed!" Winthrop fumbled in his pocket and pulled out several folded sheets.

"I don't give two hoots in hell about the mine," Slocum said. "You tried to kill me out there."

"How'd you know?"

"Nobody else still sucking air is lily-livered enough." Slocum shoved Winthrop back into the chair when the man tried to come after him. The alcohol haze was burning off fast. His eyes were bloodshot, but he started speaking more clearly.

"You'll pay for that, Slocum."

"Seems I already have. What'd you do with the silver you took from me?"

"That's all you want?"

"It'll do," Slocum said. "For a start."

"I buried it outside of town. Couldn't let anyone see me tryin' to spend those slugs. You killed them, like the marshal said?"

"That was Autumn who tried to pin the murders on me." Slocum watched the change in Winthrop's expression when he mentioned the woman. "She thought the world of you."

"What are you saying?"

"She was fighting with her sister when Summer called you some names. Autumn defended you."

"She was always my favorite. Never thought I was hers, though," Winthrop muttered.

"You two were—"

Winthrop's eyes went wide in shock.

"Hell, Slocum, she was my sister."

It was Slocum's turn to be shocked. He didn't say anything.

"They're my sisters, but they got terrible taste in men. Spring paid for it."

"What's your name?" Slocum began to realize he knew nothing about what swirled around him.

"Win Winthrop. Spring, Autumn, and Summer were all Winthrops at one time till they married."

"Winter Winthrop?"

"That's my name."

"Son of a bitch." Slocum shook his head in disbelief.

Winthrop smirked.

Slocum decided it was time to take him down a notch or two.

"They're dead."

"Spring is, but Autumn and Summer are out at the mine, fighting over what I stole away from them when they weren't looking." Winthrop tapped the papers on the table. His smirk faded when he realized Slocum was not joking.

"The mine flooded. Both were trapped inside. You might find the bodies if you pump out the lower levels, but I doubt it."

"You're lying!" Winthrop surged again, swinging at Slocum's head. Avoiding the punch was easy. Slocum shoved hard against the table and drove the edge into Winthrop's midriff, knocking him facedown onto the beer-stained tabletop.

"Where's the silver?"

"They're dead?"

"Just the latest in a long string of dead men . . . and women," Slocum reminded him. "Where'd you hide the silver you stole from me?" He thought for a moment, then added, "Where's all the silver Atkins and his gang stole? You've been slowly rounding it up, haven't you?"

"They was supposed to let me in on the robbery, but Atkins double-crossed me. Just like he did the rest of them. He recruited that feeble-minded fool Joe."

"Where's the silver? This the last time I'm going to ask. You said it was hidden outside of town. Where?" Slocum considered the stretch of road between the Silver Chalice and Tombstone. A hundred good places suggested themselves to him, and someone like Winthrop, who had been in town longer, could find a hundred more. It would take a lifetime of searching before he could unearth the treasure. Hell, it would be worse than hunting for the Lost Dutchman Mine up north in the Superstitions.

"Right at the junction of the road and the trail running to the mine."

"The Silver Chalice?"

Winthrop's head bobbed like it was mounted on a spring. All trace of drunkenness was now burned away.

"I'm going to see if it's there. If it's not, you won't be able to run far enough. I'm fed up with you and your sisters and everything about Tombstone."

"It doesn't matter what you think, Slocum." Winthrop's voice took on an edge now. "I don't care what you think." He pushed himself back from the table and wiped the blood off his nose where it had smashed into the table.

"You think you're man enough? I don't." Slocum slid the six-gun on the table toward Winthrop. "Go on. Go for it."

Their eyes locked and Winthrop flinched. He shook his head and looked away.

"That's what I thought." Slocum stood and stared at Winthrop. "You're one miserable excuse for a man. Your sisters kill themselves and all you want to do is flap around like a vulture and pick at their carcasses. You never killed them, but you waited for them to die. All three of them were more of a man than you."

"Marshal!" blurted Winthrop. But Slocum wasn't so easily duped. Winthrop's eyes went to the gun, not the doorway.

His Colt Navy caught just a little on the waterlogged holster, but Slocum still got his smoke wagon out and firing before Winthrop could raise his. The first round hit Winthrop in the chest. He gasped but wasn't dead. Slocum corrected that with his second shot. His slug drove through Winthrop's head and snapped him back in the chair. He sprawled gracelessly, the six-gun falling from his nerveless fingers to clatter on the barroom floor.

"You want to fetch the law? Anybody?" Slocum looked around the now silent saloon. Nobody moved a muscle. The oppressive heat from outside crowded in now and caused sweat to bead on a half dozen foreheads. Or that's what they'd tell one another.

Slocum strode from the saloon and mounted. There still wasn't a peep from inside. He trotted out of Tombstone, swaddled in the heat and silence. He reached the road leading east—and toward the junction going to the Silver Chalice Mine. He had no idea if Winthrop had told the truth. He probably had, since the liquor had still dulled his arrogance then. It would take only a few minutes to search the area and find out. Slocum hoped the silver was there. If it wasn't, he didn't care. It was time to ride out of Arizona Territory and get as far away from this hellhole as possible.

Watch for

SLOCUM AND THE TEAMSTER LADY

378th novel in the exciting SLOCUM series
from Jove

Coming in August!